THE WEEKDAY BRIDE

(A Regency novel)

by

Lois Tennant

Description:

Echoes of a Regency Romance.

Lord Markham Elsworth is about to lose his family home because of a codicil to his father's will of which he was unaware! Lucinda Stanton is about to lose her inheritance and leave her sister and family without support. Somehow, it seems that, in spite of obstacles and jealous rivals, they can assist each other.

REVIEWS

"I love the Regency theme Lois Tennant uses, without all the cloying attention to romance one sometimes finds!" Lauretta James

"A very pleasant read indeed!" W. Share

CONTENTS

For Ken and Candice, with love!

Chapter 1

"Sorry I had to be the bearer of bad tidings, Mark," said the Honorable Charles Sutton, as he sat back with a sigh and sipped appreciatively from the goblet of mulled wine that had been placed beside him. He eased his back against the comfort of the armchair.

"Not your fault, Charlie," replied Lord Markham Kingsley Elsworth - Mark to his friends - as he turned away and leaned his forehead against the cold windowpane. The sharp cold of the glass was soothing and steadied the turmoil of his thoughts. He stared out at the library garden. It suddenly looked overgrown and rather grotesque at this late hour of the night. Or was it early hour of the morning? The rose bushes which were such a riot of color in the daytime were charcoal smudges and the waning new moon glinted briefly on the water-fountain beside a dark shaggy willow. Shrubs drooped like hooded figures on the silver-grey expanse of the lawns that dipped to the steely grey of the small lake. It was a still night, still and cold.

Markham Elsworth turned to glance at the ornate timepiece above the fireplace. The slightly yellowed face in its decorative walnut frame, which had always seemed to hold a smile for him as a child, was now remote and aloof. It was indeed early morning. Five minutes to two o'clock to be precise. He ran a hand through his rather thick dark hair, which caught and held the bronze sheen of the firelight.

With a short sigh he pulled closer the cord of the royal blue monogrammed night robe. He had flung it on hastily on being summoned by Smithson, his elderly butler, and told that his friend, Charles Sutton, was awaiting him in the library. He had expected the worst - death of a relative at least - for surely other news could wait until daylight!

Well, none of his relatives near or far (not that he had many he particularly knew or cared much about in either category) had met an untimely end. But, in some ways, he mused, the news could mean a kind of death, for him. He sat down and leaned back with a short sigh in the armchair he had come to regard as his favorite.

It had been the favorite of his father and his grandfather before him. Although it had never been re-covered within Mark's memory, the wine-red fabric was only slightly faded over the arms and the chair was as comfortable as ever. He stretched out a cream velvet slipper towards the fire, which had revived itself under the careful ministrations of Smithson. The firelight flickered on his firm, muscular calf, but he was not aware of the warmth of the flames as they danced in contorted shapes of orange and yellow.

Mark picked up a goblet of the warm mixture served to them by the ever-reliable Smithson and took a sip. This was more to warm his blood a little than to be sociable, for suddenly it felt as if a cold breeze had swept into this cozy room that had seemed so warm and secure a few hours before.

"You're absolutely sure, Charlie?" Markham asked in the calm, expressionless manner that even his closest friends found hard to penetrate. When he had first received the news, the Honorable Charles had noticed the sudden flash of shock and disbelief. Then Markham had turned away to look out of the window. Now he seemed to be his usual enigmatic self.

"I'm sure," replied Charles. He held his friend's dark blue gaze for a moment. "Hardly think I'd have galloped half the night on a nag that has more staying power than speed, if I weren't!"

"Of course," replied Markham with a grin that for a moment lit up his face. "Must have been quite a sight!" Then he looked intently at Charles. "I really do appreciate what you've done. It's not the safest of roads either."

"Oh, as for that, I reckoned that all cut-throats and robbers would be at home in bed on a night like this. Or, on the other hand, more startled than I, as I galloped past! Took Betsy just for comfort, though!" The Honorable Charles Sutton chuckled for a moment as he patted the bulge at his waist, which concealed, Markham realized, the ancient pistol which Charlie had inherited from his late grandfather and which he occasionally fired for practice. Charlie's round, boyish face beamed like that of a schoolboy who had just played a prank. His fair hair was in complete disarray and his light blue eyes twinkled mischievously.

Both gentlemen wore their hair slightly shorter than was the fashion: Charles, because of the unruly curls which were often the envy of the fairer sex, and Markham, because he had become accustomed to shorter hair in the heat of India and found it more practical in any event. Neither was partial to the wigs worn by the more dandified set. Both Markham and Charles regarded with secret amusement the masses of artificial hair worn by some young men of their acquaintance. Their immediate circle of friends had almost all discarded the elaborate wigs in favor of their own hair, a growing habit that had motivated the peruke-makers to send a petition to the King himself, complaining of this tendency!

"You haven't put your career in jeopardy, have you?" asked Markham with a slight frown.

"Hardly think so," replied Charlie. "Old man Wingate has no idea that I read the will. And anyway, if the worst comes to the worst, I can always tell Catherine the truth and perhaps take up Yorke's offer of a partnership. Made my mind up about that on the ride over."

Catherine Wentworth was the only daughter of the Earl of Southey, an heiress of some substance. She had declared herself utterly in love with the Honorable Charles Sutton, who was the somewhat penniless son of Lord Sutton of Bramswell Manor, a jovial old man who had had two wives and seven sons, Charles being the youngest.

Catherine's father, the Earl, did not particularly dislike young Charles, but was adamant that no fortune hunter would ever marry his daughter. As a result, much to his friends' amusement and some good-natured teasing as well, Charles Sutton had pursued the study of law and was at present articled to Mr. Cyril Wingate, of Wingate and Cummings, legal attorneys of some note, thus earning the admiration of Catherine and the grudging acceptance, to a degree, of the Earl.

"What made you read the will, anyhow, Charlie?" asked Markham, leaning forward in his chair.

"I'm not sure. Unless it was a remark that Catherine made at lunch one day about how she wondered if you were coming up for the Season. And then she wanted to know if it was true

that your half-brother, Lawrence, had inherited more than you. Seems like that's the story that was doing the rounds. Didn't mean to pry, Mark, but I was working late and on my own, so I just thought -"

"I'm grateful to you that you did read the will," said Markham quietly.

"Well, personally can't stand gossip and anyhow, I owed you one," went on Charles. "Would've been a gonner for sure that night if you hadn't fought 'em off!"

"Nonsense, my lad," said Markham with a brief smile. "I enjoyed the exercise." He recalled for a moment the incident to which Charles was referring. They had come out of a gaming house in a none too savory part of London, having visited it with a friend who gambled heavily and intended spending the entire night within its precincts. Having tried unsuccessfully to persuade their friend to call it a night, they had eventually excused themselves. It was fairly late and the streets were ill-lit. The doorways of the dark stone buildings were shadowy and a mist had begun to roll in off the Thames. Putting their collars up to protect themselves against the dampness, they had stepped out into the street, intent on finding a cab of sorts. Heads down against the drizzle, they had failed to see shadows dislodge themselves and swiftly and silently come up behind them. As rough hands grabbed their shoulders, they realized that they had been set upon by at least four brigands, who had the express intention of relieving them of their money and any other valuables. Markham had struck one or two lucky blows, as he said later, and then had lifted up the fallen Charles and ducked into a doorway with him.

It must have been their lucky night, as the doorway belonged to Mother Bellarona, a somewhat infamous owner of a brothel. The door opened to Markham's touch. His eyes widened slightly at the sight before him. Ladies of doubtful virtue reclined in various states of undress on couches against the wall, some of them already giving their undivided attention to the men beside them. The atmosphere was unpleasantly warm and smelled of cheap perfume. Markham took a deep breath and was contemplating a swift retreat, when a rather large lady dressed in bright red, with hair as yellow as a caged canary, swept forward. It was Mother Bellarona. She saw what she determined might well be potential customers, but noting the state of the blond gentleman who was being supported by the tall, handsome one, she simply smiled graciously and helped the young men out of a side door into the next street, whispering an invitation into the ear of the tall gentleman. He grinned and saluted her gallantly. He hailed a passing cab and took Charles home to attend to his injuries.

"Can say what you like," said Charles after another taste of the wine, "saved my life good and proper. Only thing is, can't see how I can really save you in return. Damned shame it will be too, seeing as you seem to love this place," he waved one arm in the general direction of the garden outside, "and have made up your mind to be one of those boring country squires."

He peered at his friend who seemed lost in thought. The firelight danced on his rather stern profile, a profile which certain society ladies insisted must go back to the Roman generals: the classical nose, the firm, carved lips, the fine brow beneath the dark hair that curled into his neck and, of course, the depth of the deep blue eyes. "Wish I had discovered the codicil sooner," said Charles regretfully.

"You weren't to know," said Markham quietly. "Must say it was a pleasant surprise when I was told my father had left Elsworth to me," he added with a bitter laugh. "I always thought step-mother would persuade him to leave it to Lawrence."

"But you were wrong," said Charles earnestly. "Reckon he loved you and wanted you to have your inheritance same as you would have if your own mother had been alive."

"Maybe," replied Markham darkly, "but why the codicil then?"

"I don't know," said Charles. "It just said: 'If after six months of occupation, my son Markham Kingsley is not suitably and happily married and settled into the life of Elsworth, the entire property is to revert to my present wife, Amelia, and my son, Lawrence.' Funny thing, too, why Wingate didn't make it clear to you in the first place."

"It doesn't make sense," said Markham grimly. "Why should my father not trust me to look after Elsworth? I grew up here."

"Well, without trying to be difficult, Mark, you told me you didn't stay for very long after he married your step-mamma. Then you hightailed it off to India soon as you could!"

"I was thirteen when I left home," said Markham tersely. "And I stayed with my uncle, my father's eldest brother, until I went to Oxford. And as for going to India - well, I had a job of work to do there. And whatever else happened there is hardly anybody else's business!"

"Of course, Mark," soothed Charlie, " but you know the rumors that went around. And when you were supposed to be coming back with an Indian bride - well, I think that was almost too much for your father!"

"Well, I didn't, did I!" said Markham evenly. "And apart from being labeled a wicked philanderer or some such, I don't think anyone took much notice of rumors. I thought he and I were getting on better than we had for years, when he suddenly took ill -"

"You were, I could see it!" agreed Charles. "But if he took no notice of the rumors, who is to say your step-mamma did not! And he surely did not expect to pass on so suddenly. Daresay he didn't have time to change his will."

"You're probably right," agreed Markham with a short sigh. "Anyway, what's done is done," he added, his lips set in a tight line.

"Wish there was something more I could do, old boy," said Charles stifling a yawn. "Thing is, matter of three days till your time's up. Tomorrow, no, today - is Monday," he said glancing at the clock. "That leaves you with today, Tuesday and Wednesday. Can't see myself what female will marry on an ordinary weekday. Catherine says it's totally not done. Thought she might marry me on her birthday, you see -. " His voice trailed off and he rubbed his eyes sleepily.

"You get off to bed, Charlie," said Markham. "We can talk again in the morning - later, that is. Smithy!"

"Yes, milord," replied Smithson who materialized out of the shadows.

"Show Mr. Sutton to the room you have no doubt prepared."

"Yes, milord. This way, sir."

"Thanks Smithson," said Charlie, rising stiffly. "See you in the morning, Mark - or rather, later on today! And don't worry - remember our scrapes at college. Always got out of them somehow!"

"Thanks, Charlie. Sleep well." Markham watched his friend walk rather unsteadily out of the room and up the stairs, following the flickering candles that Smithson carried. Poor Charlie, he would feel really stiff and sore when he woke. Quite a ride he must have had, on a road that could be treacherous at night with its surface uneven in parts and the deep ruts carved in by carriage wheels in wet weather. It had probably taken him two hours in the dead of a cold spring night with only a sliver of a moon for light. Just as well he had known how to pace his horse and that the animal had been sure-footed. It was also not unknown for travelers to be robbed and held up when travelling alone. He was a good friend. College scrapes were a bit different to this, though. If you had contacts and some money on hand, you could get out of most situations then.

Markham bent down and added a log to the fire. Sparks shot up with a crackle and the embers glowed deep orange. He sank down into the armchair once again, leaned back and closed his eyes.

The best surprise of his life he had called it, when he was informed that he had inherited Elsworth. Part of him had lived in the expectation of it. Another part of him had acknowledged the influence his stepmother seemed to have over his father.

He was twelve when they married. His own mother had died six months before and there had been still too much of her sweetness at Elsworth to make way for the false laughter and glitter of Amelia Torrington. His father, Sir Kingsley Elsworth, had become quite infatuated with her smiles and flattery. Only he, the young awkward son, had had to endure the scornful glances when he made a mistake, the sharp tongue when his father was not there. He had not yet dealt with the ache in his heart for the mother he had loved so dearly and the unkindness of his step-mamma when his father was absent, had swirled like a tempest within him.

He had tried to tell his father, who would not listen. Then when a diamond clasp belonging to Amelia had suddenly been 'discovered' in his room, he had told his father that he wished to go and live with his cousins. His father had assured him that he was not being suspected of the theft, but he had left anyway. It must have hurt his father. He realized that now. And his own jealousy when another son was born had widened the rift even further. His father had another wife and another son. He was not needed.

At Oxford, he had enjoyed the life of a typical student, but contrary to many of his contemporaries, had decided to give enough time to his studies, so that he could attain some independence from a family that did not particularly seem to show an interest. He had returned home for brief holidays during the years, but made sure always to invite a friend, so that he did not have to endure personal confrontations with his father or Amelia.

After Oxford he had taken some interest in the Foreign Office. He had worked for a few years in the London offices, involved in the interpretation of the policies of the Empire.

However, he had longed to see some of the places that were merely names on a map to him and he had willingly taken up a post in India as an assistant to Sir Edward Lake, who had been appointed by the British Government to investigate the activities of certain East India Company officials. The latter were conducting private trading with the local people and enriching themselves to a remarkable degree. The situation was becoming totally out of hand. Sir Edward, however, was more concerned that Markham report on the political intrigues in Central and Northern India where with help from the French, the notorious Hyder Ali, an exceptionally capable buccaneer, was trying to secure a kingdom for himself.

Markham found the position challenging and it gave him the opportunity to travel extensively. He let it be known that his travels were ostensibly aimed at getting to know some of the customs and ways of the subjects of His Majesty. In reality he was reporting on any unrest or signs of rebellion which could affect the British position in those areas.

He smiled to himself then, recalling the balmy days in the northern province. He had spent some weeks there, letting it be known that he was studying the rituals and beliefs of an isolated Hindu cult in the foothills surrounding Najibabad. In reality, he had received information on the activities of the infamous and rather warlike Hindu tribesmen, the Mahrattas, in the surrounding district. The local inhabitants, however, refused to admit to any knowledge of these men, and if there were any present, they obviously did not regard a lone Englishman as a particular threat.

It was there he had met Krani Rajsingh, and through him, his sister, Sakina. Krani had come across Markham at the village market place where he was examining the local produce with a view to providing for his evening meal, and had been proud to display his knowledge of the English language, learned at the local mission school. He had offered Markham the hospitality of his home, quite sure that his father would not object.

Rather weary after a day's journey through the foothills on the back of a recalcitrant mule, in his opinion, a cousin of the Mongolian wild horse, Markham had gratefully accepted the offer.

He was happy not to have to pitch a tent for the night, where he would anyhow have to sleep with one eye open, his so-called guides having their own mysterious agendas when night fell. So Markham had accompanied the likeable young man. It was obvious from their home that Krani's family was of some standing in the community. White walls, cool courtyards and splashing fountains were a haven from the heat of the day and Markham looked about him appreciatively. He was assigned his own private room with a servant to tend to his needs. Markham enjoyed the hospitality and the novelty of being waited on hand and foot. This was a decided contrast to his journey so far, where he had been very independent in attending to himself and even to his own meals, bartering for edible-looking food whenever he came to a village.

The following morning, Krani introduced Markham to his sister, Sakina; Sakina of the long, dark, flowing hair, the lithe, supple body, the dark, mysterious eyes. Her unconscious beauty was a delight to Markham, who was accustomed to the formality and rigidity of English society. The silky *saris* which she wore with such grace, their bright colors making her look like an exotic creature from another world, fascinated him. Not here the stiff, starched skirts and heavy petticoats of the young ladies in London. Sakina had a freedom of movement and lightness of foot that made her seem almost mystical. She, too, had a slight smattering of English and what she could not say, she mimed, her eyes twinkling with mischief.

One morning, after he had spent about a week with them, she beckoned him with a dimpled smile of invitation to accompany her and her friends into the hills. He had no hesitation in going, as they were adequately chaperoned by one of the older women who lived in their home. He watched them gather flowers and fruit for an obscure deity. He watched them dance the ritual dance in a small clearing under the trees. He sat entranced in the shade beside the older woman as the five girls swayed and moved almost hypnotically, offering libations to the god or gods. The older woman poured a sweet liquid into a small cup and each girl took a sip. It was Sakina who held it before him and he drank too.

When they had finished and turned to go, he waved them away and continued to sit deep in thought. Why should he go back to a father who did not really want him, to a country that

lacked the spirituality that he found here? What was his destiny? His mind seemed to swirl in a warm, relaxed circle.

He heard a rustle beside him and looked up to see Sakina, an unreadable expression on her face. Then, as he watched, she continued to dance once more. This time her eyes did not leave his face and as her body moved sensuously, he did not need anyone to interpret the invitation. She twirled and swayed to an unwritten tune and stretched her arms to the sky and twirled again, her skirt lifting like a melody to reveal her slim calves. When she knelt before him, he put out his hand to stroke her long, dark hair and the leafy ground was soft and cool beneath them.

He knew now that he had fallen under her spell and that there had been something potent in the drink he had been given, for a while even forgetting the commission he had, forgetting the reason for his visit to these remote villages. He could also feel the heady effects of the mixture she had handed to him to drink. The rest of her friends, including the old lady, had somehow disappeared from sight!

Her father, according to Krani, and to judge by his attitude, continued to welcome him and treated him with respect, even with good humor. Housing a foreign guest gave him some standing in the community, and was perhaps even a safeguard against attack by the Mahrattas. Markham did not think beyond the morrow. Each day wove a hypnotic web around him and he wondered where Sakina was.

Then something had gone terribly wrong. One warm afternoon, there was a visit from an important relative and the next morning, Sakina had gone. Krani explained or tried to explain to the frantic Markham that this was a family matter. Sakina had been 'married' at birth to a distant relative whose uncle had now come to claim her. She had refused to go and had run away in the night with her childhood sweetheart, the man she had loved since she was a girl.

"Childhood sweetheart? What man is this? What about me?" Markham asked Krani, his heart a shaft of pain inside him.

"You are our guest," Krani said with a shrug. "She has always loved Rahadira. Now, you say you can get place for me in this Oxford College you talk of?"

Rahadira! The young man with the broad shoulders and slim hips who was in charge of the Rajsingh stables, where Sakina's father bred horses. Perhaps that explained Sakina's constant concern for and care of the young foals, often being seen to check on them and adamantly refusing that he accompany her!

And he was merely a guest – a political pawn, no doubt. Had Sakina merely been curious about this Englishman from across the seas, or had she been asked to keep him fascinated so that he was not aware of what was going on? Without replying, Markham had got up, packed his bags and left. Sir Edward made no comment about his prolonged absence, beyond saying that he hoped he was well. He accepted with interest the meticulous reports which Markham had compiled since leaving, and did not think it strange that the account of Markham's stay in one of the villages was somewhat brief and terse. He noted, however, that Markham looked rather drawn, and would have recommended that the young man take some well-earned leave, had not Markham insisted he was not yet ready to return to England. Sir Edward then, with a characteristic shrug, outlined another assignment which kept Markham in India for the rest of that year, this time visiting the coastal areas where most of the traders were. Markham grimly lost himself in his work and tried to think no more of the weeks that had passed, forever, it seemed.

And there might have been no rumors at all had not Krani turned up at the Embassy one day, looking for Markham. To Markham's absolute distress, he had with him a rural 'nanny', who was carrying a tiny bundle! Krani explained quite calmly that this was Markham's baby daughter of three months. The family had wanted to drown her at birth, but the nanny had snatched the child and fled. She had pleaded with Krani to find the child's father - the lovely child with the dark blue eyes, who would never be accepted here in India. Markham had chosen to go into training mode to deal with a crisis and had installed the nanny and child in a small set of rooms, giving her sufficient money for sustenance.

He needed time to think! In the meantime, Krani had tea with Sir Edward's wife, Lady Margaret Lake. Lady Margaret loved nothing better than a good bit of gossip, of which she could write to her friends back in London.

When he returned to London a year ago, encouraged by the determination of his assistant, Corporal Biggs, who bribed the captain of the ship so that they could take the child from the nanny who had already expressed her wish to return to her family, his reputation had gone before him.

He had been spying for the British Government it was said, and he had been very friendly with the locals of India. Whether for political or personal reasons it was not known, but they had it on good authority that he had been very friendly with one lady in particular! Most conservative mothers tried to keep their daughters out of his company. Markham Elsworth had a dark, mysterious side to him and he had consorted with the foreigners! He was best avoided.

This, however, only served to make him more interesting to the daughters! His tanned good looks and athletic physique produced many a coquettish whisper. Markham remained distantly polite, his heart still buried in the mystical rolling hills of India.

Then his father, Kingsley Elsworth, had died suddenly six months ago and he had come into the Elsworth Estates and into the title, making him Lord Elsworth. The estates were in a fairly reasonable financial state he discovered, after discussions with his father's fiscal officer. The tenants seemed to be self-sufficient and contented, if somewhat backward in their concept of farming. Most of them had had to adjust to the system of enclosure, which meant that communal land around the village had been replaced by individual ownership.

They had not been able to make a living on the small fields allocated to them by the Justice of the Peace and had opted for tenancy on the larger Elsworth estates. Lord Elsworth, Markham's father, had been sensitive to their plight. They retained their small strips of land, but helped farm the fields of the estate, with the promise of a share of the harvests, albeit a small share.

The little village of Elsford, three miles from Elsworth Towers, was as neat and friendly a village as one might hope for when one was almost a stranger. It boasted an inn, the Elsford Arms, neatly kept and much enjoyed by the men of the village on a holiday or after a day's labor. A short row of shops supplied necessities and the local smithy was reliable and efficient. A small church with its adjacent parish school and the doctor's house ran down the opposite length of the main street, which was shaded by ancient oaks, planted, it was believed, by some Elsworth ancestor.

Markham's stepmother, Amelia, was left a generous income and an amount of money with which to purchase a home of her own in a fashionable part of London. It was well-known that Lawrence would inherit an estate from his maternal grandmother as soon as he attained his majority, so no doubt, Markham's father had been content with his younger son's prospects.

Not that Lawrence seemed to show any interest in his future inheritance and Amelia had been heard to remark that there would be no title attached to the property from his grandmother. In any event, it seemed that Lawrence preferred to stay with his mother and spend time with his foppish friends who had never done a hard day's labor among them. Thus Amelia and her twenty year-old son, Markham's half-brother, took up residence in London and proceeded to enjoy the social calendar, something Markham's father had shrugged off as being a boring pursuit. Markham was only too glad to leave London then, in spite of the attentions of the beautiful widow, Celestine Garrick.

He had managed to bring Biggs and his daughter (whom he had decided on the spur of the moment to name Susan), one dark night back to Elsworth Towers from the room in which he had temporarily housed his child with a nurse in London. He had sent a message to his old butler, Smithson, and Smithson had prepared the South Wing. The old man had not uttered one word of criticism and had proved to be quite inventive in organizing a nursery. He had the strictest of instructions to allow no one else near that wing and, in fact, an inter-leading door was permanently locked.

Then Smithson had contacted his sister, who was middle-aged and had been a nurse, to consider the position of nanny. She had understood how much it meant to her brother and his beloved Lord Markham, and had also been very grateful for the generous monetary imbursement which would provide for her retirement years.

These past six months had been the most challenging of Markham's life. He had no fear of the child being discovered, as he knew that many in the village still saw members of the military, in Indian garb, bring dispatches to the Estate when his advice was called upon by the Foreign

Service. He would have to reveal the truth at some stage, later, but in the meantime, there could be many explanations!

Markham moved restlessly in his chair. He had also thrown himself into the upkeep of the Estate, and had hardly seen the child, trying his best to peep in at the little sleeping bundle at least twice a week.

First there had been the project to improve the sloping fields which were open to the elements and where the soil did not seem to retain moisture. He had been the target of considerable skepticism from the tenants at first, but he had seen it work in India. Irrigation canals, the addition of leaves and dry grass to the soil and plowing along the contour of a hill, could be of such benefit to intensive farming. Now, six months later, even old man Hind greeted him cheerfully when he went to inspect the progress.

His next project, rotational cultivation, was just underway. The tenants were accustomed to the open-field system, where a field would be left fallow for one year in every three or four. Markham had, however, become fascinated by the farming methods of Lord Townsend, affectionately nicknamed 'Turnip Townsend', who advocated planting turnips or grasses in the fallow field to alternate with cereals. As a result no land was left unproductive for any length of time.

Markham had called a meeting of all the most efficient farmers on his land and in the district. They had shuffled rather self-consciously into the church hall some five months before and had darted almost suspicious glances at the new Lord Elsworth, who, it was said, had spent time in India. But he appeared to be no nabob and was dressed as ordinarily as one of them. His father had been a reasonable man and they were, therefore, prepared to listen to what he had to say.

Markham had chaired the meeting, but had encouraged participation and discussion, deferring very often to the older, more experienced farmers. Mutual respect grew. It seemed they had common goals. Together they had decided on a system of fertilizing the fields, using lime and manure. Their aim was to replace the rather inferior crops of rye that they had been content to produce over the years, with wheat of a good quality. Markham had been reading as much as he could on the subject and books and articles from journals lay in neat piles on his library table.

But now, in three days' time, all those dreams might have to remain dreams! If he had to give up Elsworth Estates because some fusty old lawyer had omitted, either deliberately or by mistake, to read him the codicil to his father's will, he would make sure somebody paid for it!

Markham got up abruptly. He walked over to the window once again. The morning sky was beginning to lighten to a pale lilac-grey. He looked out over the rose garden to the smooth lawns that dipped down to the duck pond and the park. He loved this place. This was his home. It held memories of his beloved mother and also of his father. And now to lose it, because he was not yet married!

Beyond the hill curled a spiral of smoke: a tenant's cottage was awakening to the crisp new day. What plans he had too, to improve the cottages! Attention to the livestock was also a priority. He had the capital to introduce new improved strains of cattle and sheep and had been corresponding with the Earl of Leicester in this regard. The Earl was a keen and progressive agriculturist, having taken over the management of his own estates. Now all this hinged on a marriage certificate!

Irony indeed. He could have been married at least three times over to judge by the number of times old gentry with reduced fortunes who did not mind their daughter being married to someone of a questionable character, had cast pertinent hints. Lord and Lady Dillbury had practically insisted that he call on them at every opportunity, much to the dismay of their daughter. She was actually a perfectly normal, well-mannered girl. It was, however, easy to see that her affections for a certain soldier of their acquaintance could not be overlooked.

Then there were the Welton twins, all empty-headed prattle. He suppressed a shudder. They had, in fact, thrown him into the company of Celestine Garrick. He had always enjoyed Celestine's company. She was even the kind of person who would marry him in the middle of the week, just for a lark. He smiled wryly when he thought of her dark good looks and quick wit. Pity he had found her in very intimate circumstances with Ramsey Courtell one stormy afternoon when he had called at her house unexpectedly, to escape the storm.

Then there was, of course, Lady Melissa Jordan, whom hostesses had of late seated him beside, considering them 'a striking couple'. No doubt the whispers about Melissa having been involved with a peer of the realm who was already married, had suggested to the hostesses that two sullied reputations might deal well together! Melissa was at present doing the Grand Tour. What would her reaction be to a sudden proposal, he mused. No doubt they would have to elope. Her mother, ever with an eye to her position in society, would never agree to a quick wedding. Pomp and ceremony were vital to her. And, more importantly, how would Melissa and her mother react to Susan!

Melissa was perhaps the only possibility, the only person he might consider spending the rest of his life with. She was very striking with her blond hair and blue eyes and was always becomingly attired. Moreover, she seemed to find his company amusing and wherever he went she seemed to materialize at his side. At least he would never be lonely! And if her conversation was not of the intellectual variety, well, most women were not like his mother had been, with her interest in art and literature and even politics. Most women he knew confined themselves to discussions of fashion, the latest scandal or other superficial topics.

Melissa had a somewhat shady past, but then, so did he. Of course she would refuse to live in the country, which would suit his situation with the child. But, perhaps a few months at a time of her company would suffice. But, why even speculate? Where would one find her at such short notice? She was probably enjoying the attractions of Paris or on some gondola in Venice. He had to face it. He was in a fix.

There was a tap at the door. It was Smithson, carefully carrying in a large tray.

"What's that you've got there, Smithy?" asked Markham in rather depressed tones.

"A good breakfast to cheer you up, milord!" replied the old man firmly as he place the tray on the coffee table in front of the fire. "Coffee, milord?"

"Thanks, Smithy," replied Markham absently.

"You will excuse my mentioning it, milord," said Smithson standing straight and dignified beside the tray.

"What is it, Smithson?" asked Markham with a slight frown.

"We - er - should be most unhappy if Lady Amelia and young Lawrence were to return to Elsworth." The old man gave a sniff and lifted his chin defiantly.

"Have you been eavesdropping again, Smithson?" said Markham leaning over to take a slice of crisp toasted bread.

"Not really, milord," replied the old man, a faint pink blush stealing across his cheeks.

"Well, you obviously heard something," said Markham with raised eyebrow. "I'm afraid, Smithson, the law is a snake at times."

"You may scotch the snake, milord!" replied the old man.

"Oh, quoting Shakespeare at me now, are you?" said Markham with mock severity.

"Yes, milord. Just remember, as the idiom goes: he who hesitates, is lost!" With that, the stately old man turned and walked steadily out of the room, head in the air.

"Smithy!" called Markham irritably. "What on earth are you on about?"

"Here, milord," replied Smithson as he rapidly re-entered the room. "Just this, milord, begging your pardon, but I think I might know of a way out of your difficulties!"

"And what might that be, Smithy?" asked Markham, mildly suspicious, as he absently bit into the toast. Somewhere in his mind he recalled that Smithy's advice usually ended in a lecture of sorts.

Smithson had been the butler at Elsworth as long as Markham could remember. His mother had often said to him when he was growing up: "You must pay attention to what Smithson says, Markham, he is a wise man!" Markham had impishly hidden behind her skirts and mimicked her, knowing full well that Smithson could not bat an eyelid with the eyes of his mistress upon him! Later he played the game of hiding from Smithson, convinced that he would take revenge. Smithson always strove to look suitably threatening. This usually ended with Markham running to cook for support and, of course, something delicious from the pantry.

"If you would be so good as to come over to your work table, sir," said the butler, leading the way to a table that stood in one corner beside rows of bookshelves. On its surface was what might appear to be a child's game, but which was in fact a scale representation of Elsworth Estates, worked on by Markham in the long winter nights when he had first taken over the land.

Each house, each building, was represented by a small wooden block and carefully labeled. Each field was marked and the river with its twists and turns, had been molded by his lordship from bits of pottery clay that was in abundance near the pond.

"There, milord!" said Smithson triumphantly, placing a gnarled finger on a rather larger block that nestled in the bend of the river on the border of the estates.

"What do you mean, there!" said Markham with a frown. "Are you suggesting I buy Hedgeland Manor and start all over again?" He gave a short snort of derision. "Really, Smithy, I may be young enough at three and thirty years, but I want a solution which helps me stay right where I am!"

"Just so, milord," said Smithson smugly. "I was not suggesting that you buy it, but rather that you take control of it as well by marrying the owner!"

"Indeed! From what I heard, Sir Henry Stanton left it to a do-gooder niece who is rather long in the tooth and keeps chickens!" said Markham with a derisive chuckle.

"It belongs, milord," went on Smithson carefully, mindful of the fact that he must choose his words if he was in any way to save his lordship and all the rest at Elsworth Towers from the 'witch of all witches' as he privately called Lady Amelia, "it belongs to Lady Lucinda, daughter of the younger brother of the late Sir Henry. She is not long in the tooth as you put it, perhaps some 5 or 6 years your junior, in fact. She and her sister were raised by Sir Henry when their parents died in a carriage accident when the girls were still very young. Lady Lucinda was like a mother to her younger sister and ran the household most efficiently as soon as she was out of the schoolroom."

"So I must marry this efficient motherly housekeeper to save us all! What does she look like, Smithson, a cook and bottle-washer in one? With an ample bosom and rough hands, no doubt! And I must simply ride over as soon as it is light and propose that she marry me within four days! Why would she do that, Smithson? Why would any woman in her right mind do that?"

"As to why, milord - when her uncle died six weeks ago, he left her the property and a pile of unpaid bills. She could sell, but her sister and husband plus two impossible brats decided to stay on after the funeral. They are in poor straits themselves. The husband is some kind of artist. She is desperate, milord!"

"And your informant?" Markham asked shrewdly.

"I HAVE AN ER- ACQUAINTANCE of some years' standing who is housekeeper at Hedgeland Manor," said Smithson airily, reddening slightly.

"You have a lady-friend, Smithson?" said Markham with a grin. "Is that it?"

"If you say so, milord," replied the butler.

"So you and your lady-friend discuss our private affairs, do you!"

"No, indeed milord!" replied Smithson stiffly. "If you will excuse my saying so, milord, you have hardly had any affairs to discuss until this morning!"

"All right, Smithy," said Markham, with a twinkle as he looked at the old man before him. "Thank you for your concern. I will um- think on it." He walked back to the breakfast tray and absently picked up a bunch of grapes.

Smithson looked at Lord Elsworth for a long moment, gave his head a quick shake and proceeded to pour him a cup of steaming coffee. Then he gave a short bow. Just before he left the room he stopped and said: "And, as for appearance, milord, I believe she does not look like a housekeeper at all, but is tall and slim with green eyes and dark red hair which is the envy of many a maiden!"

Markham paused, a grape between his teeth, and smiled inwardly. Trust old Smithy to have a parting shot. He was a determined old fellow. Probably thinking of his own skin if Amelia and company returned. He would no doubt be turned out.

Markham bit into the grape but hardly tasted the sweetness that was awash on his tongue. Green eyes and red hair and grew up next door. Suddenly Markham frowned to himself. He had once seen a child like that. He was only about thirteen at the time. He'd gone to fish at the waterfall. There in the pool he had seen a child swimming, totally naked, her long hair floating behind her as she sang to herself. He had just stood and stared. Then she had noticed him.

"Pray, who are you?" she had asked him, her wet eyelashes blinking at him out of a pert freckled face, her bare head and shoulders just above water. He had told her. "Well, I am a water-sprite," she had declared, "and this is my pool! Go and fish somewhere else!" He had laughed at her, not unkindly though, for she was, after all, just a child of seven or eight.

"Certainly Miss Water-sprite!" he had teased. "But if you swim lower down the river, I shall catch you with my hook, haul you out and feed you to the crows!" She had looked at him uncertainly for a moment, then had grinned a toothless grin where her front teeth were changing and ducked under the water. He had just seen a flash of her little bare bottom and then had wondered off to do some serious fishing. Girls! He had no time to waste on them.

Could Smithy's paragon of virtue be the water-sprite? The little face had not been unpleasant, but one could never tell. The years changed people. Markham picked up his coffee and helped himself to another slice of toasted bread. Ah well, one must live in hope, he supposed. He would finish his breakfast, get dressed, check on the animals, and perhaps take a ride. Perhaps along the river. Perhaps even as far as Hedgelands. He wondered wryly what lengths he would have to go to in order to save Elsworth.

Chapter 2

Lucinda Stanton (or rather, Lady Lucinda Kyle Stanton, to give her full title) tossed and turned. She felt as if she had hardly slept a wink all night. Her usually cozy, downy bed suddenly seemed full of lumps and bumps and her feet felt as cold as ice.

With a sigh of exasperation, Lucinda pushed back her bedclothes, wrapped a warm woolen cloak around her shoulders and stared with eyes that felt as if they had pieces of grit in them out of her bedroom window. The sky was beginning to turn an interesting shade of lilac. In the meadow beyond the garden a young foal, the latest addition to her stable of three, was already kicking up its heels and galloping playfully in the crisp morning air.

If I could turn the clock back, thought Lucinda, I would have been out there ready for a gallop. Then a quick cup of tea with old Nan Smythe. And perhaps a chat with her husband, Will, about his crops or the sheep he was keeping. Then a fast gallop across the fields and past the woods. Sometimes she had ended up at the Thackeray's cottage.

She pressed her lips tightly together as she saw in her mind's eye the image of Joe Thackeray. She remembered the first time she had ridden that way. She had spied him at the water-pump, bare to the waist, splashing cold water over his head and arms. He had not looked embarrassed on seeing her. He had just stared at her steadily, greeted her and had gone right on with his task. Lucinda felt herself blush angrily even now as she recalled the scene. She had not stayed for tea that morning, but had turned her horse and galloped away.

Joseph Thackeray, she had been told, was quite a catch in the eyes of the village girls. He was well-built, owned his own piece of ground, large enough to be self-supporting, and spent his time working, even on a Saturday when most of the other young men were 'resting' or enjoying their ale. He could also read, they said, having spent some time as a young child in the company of Parson Melton when his mother had been responsible for cleaning the rectory. Some even said that Joe's grandmother had been a squire's daughter and that

accounted for Mrs. Thackeray's slight air of superiority, even though she was a widow with just one son.

Lucinda drew the well-worn cloak more closely around her and slipped back into bed. The warmth of her body, captured in the woolen cloak stilled the sudden chattering of her teeth as she sank back upon the pillows. Her head whirled briefly with a dizzy blankness.

She sighed and burrowed further down for warmth. Here she was, Lady Lucinda Stanton, aged twenty-seven, spinster, with a problem that seemed to have no solution.

Her mind drifted back over the last few months. She had kept house for Uncle Henry cheerfully enough after her sister, Millicent, had married, involving herself in charity work at the vicarage. Parson Melton had since retired and the young couple who now occupied the old stone house, were enthusiastic and friendly. The Reverend Arthur Collins and his wife, Jenny, had become more than just acquaintances. Jenny was only twenty-one, but a delightful young woman and a perfect foil to her rather more serious husband. He was a young man who regarded his chosen profession as a God-given calling where care for your neighbor played an important part and where the poor, particularly children, were not simply to be left to their lot in life, especially not to the workhouse! He and his wife encouraged their parishioners to care for the needy in their own community. Some skeptical folk, unwilling to change their selfish ways, dubbed him a Wesleyan, but in an eloquent sermon he had silenced them, quoting directly from scripture to prove that each one of them should be taking to heart the teachings of the Savior they professed to follow.

The early morning rides had become something she looked forward to. She had always enjoyed the freshness, the uncomplicated treasures of nature which reached out to one, and, if she was to be truthful, she had looked forward to seeing Joe. He had looked at her with warmth in his eyes. He might just be a small farmer, but he was quite good company, she had thought. Mrs. Thackeray was pleasant enough. She had even once hinted to Lucinda over one of their cups of tea, that if Joe ever decided to marry, she would move out and stay with her sister on the other side of the village. Joe had often spoken of building onto their house should he marry. His children would not grow up in a cottage!

She remembered the times Joe had helped her into her saddle, his strong brown arms lifting her as if she were as light as the air! Her feminine instinct had told her that there was a gentle awareness between them. How naïve she had been! What a romantic fool!

For some unknown reason, Uncle Henry had not liked Joe. Called him a 'young upstart' who did not know his place. In fact, he had once warned Lucinda not to become too friendly with the Thackerays. They were just common farming stock for all their airs. Lucinda had ignored the advice, largely because Uncle Henry did not pay much attention to his neighbors or his tenants. How could he judge people he hardly knew?

Lucinda had saddled Firefly as usual early one morning six weeks ago. She had given him his head and he had followed a familiar path. The clip-clop of Firefly's hooves brought Joe Thackeray from the barn where he had been working. His shirt sleeves were rolled up to the elbow. He stood with his hands on his hips as he watched Lucinda approach.

"Good morning!" she called cheerfully. "Is your mother home?"

"Morning," Joe replied with a mock salute. "No – old Mrs. Jardine's been taken poorly. Ma was called out 'fore sunrise."

"Oh," replied Lucinda, noticing as she came closer that his shirt was unbuttoned and carelessly tucked into his work trousers. A mat of light brown hair sprang from his chest. She paused for a moment. She knew she should be on her way.

Then Joe made her decision for her. He stepped forward and took hold of Firefly's reins. "Daresay I can make a cuppa as good as Ma," he said as she slid from the saddle. With a

slight smile he looped the reins over a post and led the way into the cottage with its cleanly scrubbed steps and bright floral curtains.

Lucinda followed. It was, she acknowledged, not quite the thing for a young lady to do, but this was a friend, an old friend.

Once inside, she took off her hat and gloves and watched as Joe stoked up the fire and the kettle began to simmer. He whistled tunelessly as he worked.

"Let me," said Lucinda and set out two cups and saucers from the rack where Mrs. Thackeray kept her cups hanging in shining order. By now the water was almost on the boil. Lucinda put out her hand to lift the teapot to find that Joe had done the same. She pulled away with a laugh. "Sorry!" she said.

"Not as sorry as I am," said Joe, retaining his hold on her hand.

"Joe? Why do you say that?" she asked quickly, her breath catching in her throat as she tried to pull her hand free.

"Don't try your upstart airs on me, Lucinda," Joe almost growled as Lucinda looked at him in astonishment. "I am just as good as he is!" With that he jerked her towards him and she felt his powerful arms crush her against himself. Then his mouth came down on hers in a hard demanding kiss and his tongue forced itself between her lips.

"Let me go immediately, Joe Thackeray!" gasped Lucinda as she squirmed free.

"So, you've got a temper to match that hair!" said Joe with a short laugh as he watched her face flame angrily.

Lucinda glanced around quickly. There was only one door to the outside, and Joe had his back to it! "What's the matter with you!" she said angrily. "If my uncle hears of this -!"

"Your bloody uncle!" said Joe darkly. "What do you think it was like to hear George Bistow tell my mother yesterday afternoon that you and he had almost set a date! It's what your uncle wants! What do you think it was like to hear him talk of all his visits to the Manor! What's an old man's kiss like, Lucinda?" he said with a sneer. "And what else have you allowed him to do? If I think of how I could not wait just to touch your hand and all the time you and he..." Joe slammed a large fist on the kitchen table so that the cups rattled and shook in their saucers.

"You don't know what you're saying!" gasped Lucinda.

"Don't I?" said Joe grimly. "Can you deny that he visits regularly?"

"No, but ..."

"Can you deny that you've let him kiss you!"

"Joe, you don't understand! He visits my uncle! He's much older than I am!" said Lucinda desperately as he took a step closer.

"Can you deny that your uncle has debts and that Bistow has plenty of money?" he breathed, his face close to hers, his hands rough on her shoulders.

"How dare you say that!" said Lucinda coldly, a deadly calm now replacing her anger. "What right do you have to interrogate me?" She twisted under his arm and put the table between them. For a moment the only sound was the insistent rattle of the lid of the forgotten kettle as the water boiled and hissed beneath it.

"I should take you out to the barn right now and teach you a lesson you'll never forget, my lady!" said Joe with a sneer on his lips. He leaned over the table. Lucinda backed away, but the heat of the fire was behind her.

"What – what do you mean?" she stammered, a cold chill creeping up her spine in spite of the hearth behind her.

"I don't think you're as innocent as you look!" said Joe darkly as he began to advance around the table towards her.

Lucinda's legs felt weak and she could not move. "Joe, please," she began.

Suddenly he reached out for her and jerked her towards him. She stifled a scream as she felt his warm breath on her neck. She must talk to him! Remain calm! Now he began to kiss her in the region of her ear, her throat. She felt the rough stubble of his beard against her cheek. She pushed her hands against his immovable chest. Swiftly he grabbed her hands and held them behind her.

"Joe – don't!" she begged desperately as he began to fumble with the buttons of her blouse.

"Don't what?" he asked thickly as he ripped the buttons open.

With her last bit of remaining strength, Lucinda screamed and bit into his arm. Then she felt her feet slide from under her as he hurled her to one side with a curse. The last she remembered was a dull thud as her head struck the edge of the table.

A few seconds later, she pulled her clothing together, grabbed her hat and gloves and staggered out of the cottage. With grim determination and without a backward glance, she flung herself onto Firefly who shot forward down the avenue of trees. She clung on, sobbing.

Then having enough presence of mind, she veered towards the river and the deep, secluded pool. There she took off her torn riding habit and blouse and scrubbed herself with arum root until her skin was raw. Somehow, after she knew not how long, she managed to rearrange her torn habit, reach the Manor and run in by a side door without being seen by the few servants her uncle employed.

She changed and braided her hair. She felt numb, as if she were moving in a dream. Then she made her way downstairs, trying to act as normally as possible. She must have time to think. Must she talk to her uncle? To whom could she tell what had happened to her?

Downstairs she found the housekeeper, Sarah, wringing her hands anxiously. "Where have you been so long, Miss Lucinda? It's yer uncle, lovey. He's been taken bad."

Uncle Henry had complained of sudden chest pains that morning and Sarah's nephew had gone to fetch the doctor from Elsford. Lucinda rushed into her uncle's bedroom and kneeled at his side. He was pale and obviously in pain.

Uncle Henry clasped Lucinda's hand and with lips, which were almost blue, whispered that she pray for him. Lucinda, with tears streaming down her face, prayed the Lord's Prayer out loud, and with a sigh, Uncle Henry gasped his last just as the doctor arrived. His heart, Dr Peterson said. There was nothing anyone could have done. It was a sad time. In spite of his lack of any real interest in his property or in his tenants, Uncle Henry had been a well-known figure as he rode to the hunt or called at the village inn for a glass of ale.

Sarah Greenley, the housekeeper, who had been with the family since Lucinda and her young sister, Millicent, had come to stay after their parents' death, took control. She knew exactly what to do. But even she, Sarah, of the warm comforting arms that had so often held the two little orphan girls in the pain they had gone through, who had so often told them tales and shaken with quiet laughter at their escapades, even she could not avert what had happened since Uncle Henry's death.

Lucinda had woken many a night to find herself clinging to the bedpost after a dreadful nightmare. Luckily, even the ever-vigilant Sarah had noticed nothing amiss, putting Lucinda's paleness down to her grief for her uncle. And she had worried so. The incident with Joe Thackeray had really upset her! What lies had that awful old George Bistow been spreading about her?

Then, one sunny morning, a week after the funeral, two men in black suits and identical black hats arrived from London. They presented documents and in the kindest way possible informed Lucinda that her uncle had left her heir to the property which included Hedgeland Manor - and also, unfortunately, heir to the considerable debts he had accrued.

Debts! Lucinda was startled and disbelieving. Then, as they began to explain, her heart grew heavy within her. Uncle Henry, who had regularly once a month gone to London to "see to his affairs", had spent most of his time at a gambling establishment. Sometimes he had won, but mostly, he had lost. He had also had a lady-friend whom he had kept in great style in a house in London.

The lady had had to give up the house, they assured her, as it had not been fully paid for. But there was no money over to cover his other debts. Here was a list of them. The total sum was such that they would have to confiscate the property surrounding Hedgeland Manor and sell it to the highest bidder. The house might just escape being sold, but most of the contents (and they cast an appreciative eye over the old but well-preserved furnishings) would probably also have to go.

"But that's no use!" Lucinda cried. "We make our living from the rent of the tenants and from the fields! And what about our livestock?"

"We understand, Lady Stanton," they answered quite sympathetically, "but we have no alternative."

"When?" she asked grimly. "When will you sell our land?"

"By the end of April," they answered.

It was just ten days now until the end of the month. If she had only herself to care for, she might be able to survive. She could keep her hens, develop the garden and sell bulbs or even take in sewing in winter. And she could just keep the simplest of furnishings. All she really needed was a roof over her head. There was also a very small income which her mother had left to her as the eldest daughter. But it was not enough even to retain the servants. What would happen to Sarah and the others?

Then there was a possibility that Sybil Campbell, who ran the small parish school attached to the vicarage, might have to go and look after her mother who had fallen ill and who lived in Bath. Jenny had once asked Lucinda if she would not be interested in teaching a class. Most of the children were those of the villagers and the tenants, at least those who could be persuaded to give their children an education. There were also a half dozen from the little orphanage that Jenny had opened and which was run by a matronly widow woman. That might add to her meager income.

But then Millicent had announced after the funeral that she and Alfred Sydenham, her artist husband, were thinking of staying on for a while. The children loved it so here at Hedgelands. They had so much freedom to run around and to roam in the woods. And Sydenham felt inspired already when he looked at the light on the distant hills.

She should have known, thought Lucinda. They had arrived with an amount of luggage scarcely suited to a mere week's stay. At the time she had put it down to the fact that two little children, a boy and a girl of four and two respectively, probably needed piles of clean clothes. And, of course, Millicent had never been one for good organization.

It turned out that Sydenham had not sold many paintings over the last year and that their landlady had refused to allow any more credit. The funeral, said Millicent cheerfully, had, in fact, been a godsend. Lucinda had just looked at her sister blankly. And who were those men from London, her sister had wanted to know? Lucinda replied that they were just sorting out the legalities surrounding Uncle Henry's death.

She remembered Millicent growing up, always cheerful and carefree. She had hardly known their parents who had died when Millicent was only three years old and Lucinda was six. Even at that young age, Lucinda had felt a strong protective feeling towards her little sister with her golden curls and big blue eyes. And Uncle Henry, the childless old widower that he was, had seemed to favor her. If there were any sweetmeats over or any special surprises, they were kept for Milly. Lucinda had not minded. Milly must be cared for.

Then when Milly was nineteen, she had met Alfred Sydenham. He had been given an assignment to paint the portraits of Lady Elsworth and her son. The second Lady Elsworth, that is. The first had died of some mysterious fever. The first son had gone away, they said. Lord Elsworth had remarried.

Milly met Alfred in the village library. It was love at first sight and since then they had been together almost every day of their lives. Even Uncle Henry's misgivings and her own gentle warnings had failed to budge Milly. She had married her penniless Alfred in the little village church in the wedding dress that had belonged to their late mother. What a picture she had made, with her fair hair and bright eyes!

And to give her her due, Milly had never complained. There had probably always been enough to eat, enough for the occasional new dress and always exciting, if rather bohemian, company. Her letters had been bright and amusing, descriptions of a life quite foreign to Lucinda, of trips to Italy, of living in an attic in Paris for a while. When the children came they had settled down in a small cottage on what seemed to be an old estate on the outskirts of London. Alfred had been able to paint a great deal and had taken numerous trips into the city to sell his work, but it was a difficult way to support a family.

What bad timing for their fortunes to change now, thought Lucinda as she lay back and drowsed. Two little children and another on the way, as Milly had happily told her.

If it were not for Milly, whom she could never and would never let down, she could survive somehow. And one thing she was determined about: no-one must know what had happened to her. Joe had abused and insulted her in anger. Let that be on his conscience, if he had one! She did not want to see him or speak to him ever again! If what he had said became known in the village, she would have to go away. She would not be an object of pity or scorn! But could she trust Joe to remain silent? One day he might tell someone what George Bistow had said! What if he tried to make contact with her again? Her only hope was that he would respect his mother's feelings and keep silent.

How Lucinda longed to go far away and pretend that none of this had ever happened. She felt as if she had lost something very precious, and there was no peace within her. But could she go away now and leave her sister? What reason would she give? A friend who needed her? Perhaps she would have to talk to Jenny. She could pretend she needed to go away to start a new life. Perhaps say that she did not get along with Alfred! Poor Alfred! He was the sweetest brother-in-law one could hope to have!

And perhaps Alfred would be able to sell a few paintings again. They could stay on at Hedgeland in the meanwhile! Surely there must be a solution! She must talk to Milly -

"Oh, Sarah! Did I oversleep?" cried Lucinda as she sat up quickly in bed to the rattle of a teacup and Sarah's chuckle.

"No, my lady, the sun has hardly risen. The others are all still sound asleep. Not that I'm surprised, though," she added a little disapprovingly. "They allow those children far too much freedom. You two had to be in bed at a reasonable hour!"

"Oh, Sarah," smiled Lucinda as she sipped her tea. "that is just the way they are! How did you sleep?"

"Fair to middling, my lady," replied Sarah as she twitched back the curtains which had been half open. Sarah pursed her lips as she looked out of the window. Then she wiped her hands on her white apron and proceeded to straighten the faded yellow cushions on the window-seat.

"It sounds so strange to have you call me by my title!" said Lucinda ruefully. She had already had that argument with Sarah - and lost! "Not that having a title helps if you have no money!" she added with a sigh.

Sarah did not reply.

"What is it, Sarah?" asked Lucinda, sensing that the older woman was not merely tidying the room for want of something to do. Sarah took a deep breath and turned to face Lucinda. She looked down at this girl who had grown under her care to be a young woman. She looked at the worn cream nightdress peeping out from under the old grey woolen cloak and at the dark mass of auburn curls that lay in disorder on the pillow, at the fine green eyes, the mouth that was always ready to smile.

"You could do much worse than George Bistow, Lucinda," she said softly, for a moment forgetting the title.

"George Bistow!" said Lucinda, putting down her cup with a rattle. "What do you mean?"

"You know what I mean, my lady," replied Sarah with a gentle smile. "Your neighbor has made his intentions quite clear on a number of occasions!"

"Oh, Sarah!" exclaimed Lucinda. "You know that I never ever took him seriously. He was Uncle Henry's friend - and almost just as old! I mean he has grown sons about my age!"

"Nevertheless," said Sarah primly, "he has a beautiful home and he needs a wife to run it. He says it lacks the feminine touch since his wife died."

"When did he say that?" asked Lucinda with a frown.

"He had a word with me at the funeral. He said he would not bother you so soon after the funeral, but as he knew I had brought you up and was almost like a mother to you -" went on Sarah wiping her hands on her clean apron once again, "I should just mention his name in passing as it were."

"But I don't love him, Sarah!" exclaimed Lucinda. "And those three big sons look at me as if they would like to grab me in some dark corner!"

"Oh, my lady, how can you say that!" said Sarah agitatedly. "You could always ask him to move them out of the house if you didn't get on with them. And think of the comfort you would live in. I think he would even provide for Milly and her family until they get on their feet again. Farmer Bistow is a wealthy man!"

"But you were the one who criticized him when he came visiting, Sarah!" said Lucinda, her heart sinking within her at the thought of Farmer Bistow. "How many times did you not tell me that my late parents would have expected me to marry someone of my own station! And you said his table manners were not up to standard!"

"You know the saying, my lady," replied Sarah quietly as she took the cup from Lucinda, "beggars cannot be choosers, as it were." She paused at the door. Lucinda's heart beat rapidly. Did Sarah know? How could she know that she had once been attracted to Joe? "I would gladly give my life for you and Miss Milly, you know that, child. And I cannot bear to think of either of you being in want or having to suffer. And I know 'is lordship ain't left you exactly in the pink when it comes to money. Sarah makes it 'er business to know these things. You have a roof over your 'ead and that's about all!" Her lip quivered slightly. "You will think about what I have said, won't you, my lady?" Then she quietly closed the door behind her.

Lucinda gave a sigh of relief. Sarah did not know! But George Bistow! And he had already spoken to Sarah! Lucinda held her head in both hands for a moment and suppressed a shudder. George Bistow with his cheery round, red face, always with a dent around his temples where his hat sat too tightly; and his hands with their short stubby fingers and long ginger hair that encroached almost as far as his knuckles! He had always been pleasant enough and at times jovial, especially after an hour or two with Uncle Henry in the library where they had sat drinking port, playing cards and discussing 'business'. He was never short of money, everyone knew that, but he was at least twenty-five years older than she!

One evening he had taken her hand on leaving and held it far too long. Then he had raised it to his lips. She could still recall the soft, fleshy feeling of his lips, the cloying odor of clothes that needed a good airing. She had maintained her poise, but had hurried off to wash her hand with soap soon afterwards.

Lucinda gave herself a mental shake. She was not going to allow others to make decisions for her. She flung back the bedclothes with determination and walked across the wooden floor in her bare feet to the small threadbare wheat-colored carpet in front of the washstand. She poured water from the pitcher that Sarah had brought in with the tea. It was still warm.

Quickly she washed herself and then slipped into the riding habit that had belonged to her mother. It was a bottle green shade and had been carefully mended once or twice, but she knew that it was comfortable and gave some color to her cheeks. She had cut up the other one and the blouse that went with it and fed it into the flames of her hearth one evening when everyone was asleep.

Now she executed some energetic strokes with her hairbrush to disentangle the riot of curls. With a practiced twist she knotted her hair in the nape of her neck. She leaned forward to gaze at herself for a moment in the small oval mirror above the washstand.

Reflecting back at her were a pair of dark green eyes fringed by dark lashes, a nose that was passable for its pert shape and a few rows of light freckles that would, she knew, increase in number in the summer. Her mouth, she decided, was probably her best feature. It was perhaps a bit wide, but her lips were clearly defined and a deep natural color. Then, of course, there was her hair, which, apart from its color that could kindly be called auburn, or unkindly be dubbed 'rusty', was generally a mass of curls unless she fastened it securely. Millicent could make it look quite fetching, and no doubt, if she had a lady's maid, she would not be complaining! But what was the use of dreams now?

Lucinda dismissed her reflection with a shrug. It was no good pretending she was a beauty. She should perhaps have married by now. Uncle Henry had once promised her a season in London. He had even taken her and Millicent to visit a cousin in London one Christmas. She had been twenty years old then and Millicent, eighteen. Uncle Henry had dutifully chaperoned them to parties and two balls. They had danced until their feet ached. She could still remember the dress she had worn, pale yellow with silver trimmings. Milly's had been blue with the same trimmings. They had felt like princesses.

She had even turned down a proposal of marriage from a rather serious young blade who had declared that she was all he was looking for in a wife! His name was the Honorable Percival Coombs. He was quite good-looking in a scholarly kind of way and pleasant company, but how could she have left Millicent alone at Hedgeland Manor!

Then, ironically, Millicent had met Alfred a few months later. She sometimes wondered what had happened to Percival, if he had married. Once she had even contemplated writing him a short note just to enquire after his health, of course. But then common sense had prevailed. Had that been another lost opportunity?

But that was the past. Reality was a solution to the present problems - and preferably, please Heaven, not by marrying George Bistow!

Lucinda pulled on her riding boots, picked up her hat and quietly headed for the outer door that led from the corridor near her room. She ran lightly down the old stone steps and through the rambling garden to the stables. Within ten minutes she had saddled Firefly, and was galloping swiftly out of sight of the house along the bridle path that led past the fields.

The sun had already risen and was casting its rather feeble early morning beams on the tops of the trees. Mist clouds were scudding across the sky. It would be a lovely spring day. Lucinda breathed deeply and for a moment the sheer exhilaration of the gallop made her forget her uneasy thoughts and she gave herself to the glorious moment of fresh air and the countryside that she loved.

As the path became more uneven, Lucinda reined in the stallion and proceeded at a trot. Without really thinking, she found herself heading for the pool. It was her favorite spot and one where she could think and plan undisturbed.

When she reached the little grove of willow trees, Lucinda reined in Firefly and slid off his back, looping the rein so that he could crop the green grass that greeted the spring. She sank down on her favorite seat, a log that had fallen in the shape of a bench, and caught her breath.

If only she had come here that morning instead of going to the Thackerays! But she had trusted Joe. Had she ever really known him, though? How dared he! How dared Joe Thackeray insinuate that she had given favors to George Bistow! How dared he become so angry with her? How dared he treat her roughly like a common village girl? He might as well have taken a knife and ended her life then and there. Her life would never be the same again. She was spoiled goods for any decent man if he repeated the rumors. She sat brooding for a moment. Was she being too dramatic? Perhaps it was time to unearth some of those cousins her mother had spoken of with affection. There might be one who needed a companion or a governess of sorts. She could not face the village folk and would always find herself wondering if Joe had told anyone. She could not face seeing Joe again!

She looked up and over the pool to the trickling waterfall, the ferns dotted about with lilies, the tall hedgerows and the rolling fields beyond. Yes, she might have to leave all this, the home she knew. Her life would change. A moment of misplaced trust had changed her life forever!

Lucinda closed her eyes tightly. A tear squeezed out of her lids and trickled down her cheek. She sniffed and found the handkerchief that was always tucked into her skirt pocket. Oh, Uncle Henry, you dear old foolish man! If only, she thought, if only I had known that you were squandering money, perhaps I could have saved some for Milly. But enough of that! Self-pity took one nowhere.

What was left for her now? And what would happen to Milly and her little family?

Lucinda felt a heaviness descend on her spirit, a heaviness she had felt only once before - when her parents had died. Then Sarah had been a comfort. Now, she could not even confide in Sarah for Sarah wanted her to marry a man old enough to be her father, a man with whom she had nothing in common. She suppressed a shudder. How could she ever let a man like that get close to her!

It was a perfect morning and would be a lovely day. The pool near her feet was almost as still as a millpond, its shining eye gazing at her with its age-old wisdom with now and then a gentle ripple disturbing its surface. Here and there a hovering dragonfly skimmed the water and a water hen in the reeds on the other side clucked disapprovingly. The weeping willows had already caught the morning sun as they gracefully dipped their shaggy heads over the water.

A velvet damp nose nuzzled her neck and Lucinda jumped with an involuntary laugh. Firefly was impatient to be on his way again. Somehow the laugh made her feel better. She still had ten days in which to find a solution with regard to the sale of the property surrounding Hedgeland Manor! A lot could happen within that space of time.

She would speak to Milly - hold a family conference - yes, that is what she would do! Although she was the rightful heir, Alfred and Milly would have to be part of that decision, for it would affect their lives as well. Only then would she be able to make her own plans to go away for a while. She would express a life-long ambition to travel or visit distant relatives. There had to be a solution!

Chapter 3

And so it was with a firmer step that Lady Lucinda returned to Hedgeland Manor. She handed Firefly over to the young lad, Abe, who mucked out the stables and looked after the horses. He did it for a square meal a day and a bed in the stable loft. Then she took off her hat and seeing some movement in the direction of the parlor, decided to greet the family who seemed to have risen at last, before she went upstairs to change for breakfast.

It was thus that she stepped into the parlor from the garden, her hair in slight disarray, her cheeks flushed from the ride and her eyes bright from the new hope of the ten days still left to her.

For a moment her mouth hung open. She looked upon a family scene. Her brother-in-law was leaning back in their late uncle's chair with the benign expression of a resident lord as he nibbled on a tasty cheese scone. Her sister was seated at an occasional table pouring tea from Uncle Henry's silver teapot. The two children were sitting at her feet, quietly coloring in on paper probably provided them by their artist father. And sitting on the best couch, which was only slightly worn, was an elegant gentleman, sipping tea from Uncle Henry's best china and tickling Hannibal, the family cat, under the chin as if he had known the family for years.

Lord Markham Kingsley Elsworth looked up from his teacup. He saw framed in the doorway a tallish, slim, auburn-haired young lady, who looked hardly over the age of twenty-two or thereabouts. In her hand she swung a dark green hat that matched her riding habit – one which reminded him of the painting of his grandmother in the gallery at Elsworth Towers. That, at least, he knew: the outfit was sorely outdated. The wearer regarded him with slightly parted lips and a level stare. Could this be –

"Oh, Lucinda, there you are!" exclaimed Millicent, answering his question immediately. "No-one knew where you were! You shouldn't go out like that, my dear, galloping away out there on your own. You had us quite worried! Now do have some tea – and oh, how remiss of me! Have you met Lord Markham Elsworth?"

Lord Elsworth? Lucinda inclined her head as the same lord gently deposited Hannibal on the couch beside him. He then placed his cup and saucer carefully on the small table near him, and rose to his feet. A slight bow in her direction and she felt obliged to give him her hand in acknowledgement. He bowed again and then released her fingers. His own were smooth and cool to the touch. Hers were probably hot and sweaty from the ride!

"Delighted," he said politely. "I was just pointing out to your sister that although we are neighbors, I have unfortunately not had the pleasure of meeting you since my return to Elsworth." His lips curved in a polite smile.

Lucinda inclined her head and smiled briefly. This must be the new Lord Elsworth. She could not recall ever having met this rather impressive-looking neighbor! This must be the eldest son, returned to his inheritance. She raised her chin as she always did when she felt slightly embarrassed or challenged. She knew her hair must be a mess and she was certainly not attired for the drawing room.

"You are very welcome, Lord Elsworth," she said with only the slightest flush betraying her discomfort. "Pray be seated and enjoy your tea." She noticed how his cream shirtfront lay in perfect folds against a dark brown fitted jacket.

"Here we are, dear," said Millicent passing a cup and saucer to Lucinda who sat down as elegantly as she could on a nearby stool. The only other place was on the couch beside his lordship, a place now vacated by Hannibal, but she was not going to risk that! She probably smelt of horseflesh after her ride!

She felt an involuntary giggle rising in her throat. How ironical! Here she was, conversing with a real live eligible lord who happened to be a neighbor and she was now beyond the scope of any decent man and looked a fright! She bit her lip. It would not do to break out into hysterical laughter at this point!

Fortunately her niece and nephew chose this moment to display their drawings and both mother and father commented and admired. Lucinda found a pair of dark blue eyes fixed on her face. She raised her own eyes and lifted her chin. Need he stare!

"I believe you have some interest in modern agricultural methods, Lord Markham?" asked Lucinda, undaunted by the cool scrutiny and unable to read his expression. She racked her brain for comments she had overheard her uncle and George Bistow make. Neither of them had been very impressed, she could remember that. New-fangled ideas, as far as they were concerned, were doomed to failure! And Lord Elsworth was making himself a laughing-stock, according to them.

"I have introduced some new ideas," replied his lordship in even tones. "Do you have some interest in agriculture, Lady Lucinda?"

Was the man being facetious?

"Oh, you should see Lucy," interrupted Millicent with a laugh. "She loves to see things grow. My first memories are of us playing in this garden," she waved a graceful hand in the direction of the rose-garden just in view through the open door, "and of Lucy telling me to mind the roses and not to hurt them, they might cry! She even prunes them herself to this day!"

Lucinda took a deep breath. So now she was not only a rather disheveled neighbor, but also a rather eccentric and unladylike one! However, his lordship seemed to display merely a polite interest in her sister's remarks. To her surprise he leaned forward and addressed her directly. "Would you mind perhaps giving me some advice on roses, Lady Lucinda? I have a gardener whom I am sure is excellent with lawns, but knows very little about roses!"

"Why, certainly, milord," replied Lucinda somewhat confused as Lord Elsworth rose and made his way towards the doorway leading to the garden. "You mean, now?" she added.

"If you don't mind," he said blandly.

Lucinda rose, nodded politely and preceded him out of the door. Behind her she heard the shrill voice of her niece with a "Can I come too?" and the firm voice of Milly who had some other instructions for the child.

Lucinda led the way up the cobbled path to the rose-garden without saying a word. She had left her hat inside, so she merely smoothed her hair down as best she could. Little did she realize that the dark auburn curls that had escaped from the knot at the back of her head gave her a decidedly feminine look and glinted with deep gold lights as they caught the sunlight which danced through the trees.

"What would you like to know, Lord Markham?" began Lucinda calmly as she turned to face Markham.

"Would you forgive me if I broached another subject to you?" asked Markham as he indicated a weather-worn garden bench in an alcove covered by trailing wisteria. Dry leaves, a remnant that had not been blown away by the early spring winds crunched beneath Lucinda's riding boots as she led the way.

"As you wish," replied Lucinda, sitting down. She glanced quickly at his rather forbidding profile as he, too, sat down a short distance from her on the bench. She just hoped that her tenants were not poaching again. She remembered the last incident Uncle Henry had had with the late Lord Elsworth, the result of which had been very little contact between the neighbors for some years. Then she watched with some fascination as his lordship gently dislodged a tiny spider that had landed on the arm of his coat, no doubt spiraling down in

surprise at the invasion of its home. His long, tapered fingers were brown from the sun but moved gently as he placed the little creature on a branch nearby.

Markham took a deep breath and turned diagonally on the bench so that he was facing her. He placed one arm on the back of the bench between them and leaned forward slightly, his expression intense.

"Miss Stanton," he began, "both you and I, I believe, are at this moment facing a personal crisis."

Lucinda glanced at him quickly. "What do you mean?" she asked quickly, her heart thudding. "Who told you that?"

"I shall explain my source shortly," went on Markham. "I know this is a personal question and one I have no right to ask, but, am I correct in thinking that your late uncle has left you in financial straits?"

"You are," said Lucinda faintly, relief sweeping over her. Then she once again raised her chin and looked at him fixedly. "I daresay it will be common knowledge pretty soon. Within a week the bank will be taking my property and most of the contents of the house." Although her voice was steady, Lucinda found herself blinking away a threatening tear.

Markham nodded slightly, then looked out at the profusion of roses and shrubs for a moment as if he were collecting his thoughts. Lucinda watched him purse his lips slightly. Then he turned to look at her. "I have a proposal which might suit both of us," he said slowly.

"What kind of proposal?" asked Lucinda, her heart beginning to beat more quickly. Perhaps he would rent the property, take over the loan –

"Just what I say," he replied with the suggestion of a smile which did not quite reach his eyes as he watched her reaction carefully. "It is a proposal of marriage."

Lucinda felt her eyes widen as she drew in her breath in surprise. "Why would you want to marry me?" she asked quickly. "You know nothing about me!"

"True, and you know nothing about me," replied Markham with his inscrutable expression, "but I find myself in a position where I could lose all I have worked for –" Then he told her briefly about the codicil to his father's will and about how Charlie had ridden through the night to warn him.

"Why did they not tell you this when the will was read?" asked Lucinda with a puzzled frown.

"That is a question I have been asking myself over and over in the last few hours," said Markham grimly. "Someone was negligent or has an axe to grind!"

"So it seems! And you have to be married by Thursday! But that's impossible!" exclaimed Lucinda.

"I was hoping you might make it possible," said Markham looking at her with a serious expression. "Before you reply," he went on, as she took a breath and opened her mouth, "let me explain what you would stand to gain by the arrangement."

He paused slightly and leaned back, assuming a relaxed stance he did not feel within. "Firstly, I would be prepared to settle your late uncle's debts. Secondly, your sister and her family could remain here at Hedgelands and I would provide funds to renovate the Manor." Lucinda stared at Markham in amazement. Could she be dreaming? How often had she not longed to see Hedgelands restored! "Thirdly, I have a friend in London who would willingly organize an exhibition of your brother-in-law's paintings. Also, I should not interfere in any charitable work in which you are involved if you should wish to continue with it. Your sister tells me you are fairly involved?"

"Er – yes," replied Lucinda quite taken aback at the growing list and hardly able to think clearly.

"I would also make sure that you are financially independent and would not prescribe to you how you should spend your money as long as it is to your benefit," added Markham with a smile. This time the engaging smile reached his eyes and Lucinda had a glimpse of the charm under which many a lady had melted.

"And what do I have to contribute to all this?" asked Lucinda carefully.

"You have to agree to marry me on Wednesday," replied Markham with a slightly rueful grin. "I know that is a lot to ask, but it is the only way I can retain my right to my inheritance and outwit whoever has been trying to oust me." The inscrutable expression once again covered his handsome features.

Lucinda found herself looking at a dark curl that had found its way over the collar of his coat, a coat that was immaculate, yet casual, in a velvety fabric. His riding breeches were dark mahogany and his glossy, calf-length riding boots were a good match. There was a faint scent of gentlemen's cologne. There was no doubt that Lord Markham was a man of means.

"And once I am married?" asked Lucinda raising her chin and feeling her color rise.

"Why, we should treat each other with respect," went on Markham, kindly looking out at the rose garden as he noticed her embarrassment. "You would have Elsworth Towers to see to, although I have a good housekeeper, a butler and a number of other servants. You could engage more servants if you wished," he added pleasantly. "My gardener would love someone to take an interest in the gardens! I am more interested in the fields," he added with a short laugh, "a fact of which he never ceases to remind me!"

"You would not dismiss any of our tenants?" asked Lucinda, although she realized she was not really in any position to bargain. Her mind was swirling! Milly would be safe! She,

herself, would be safe! She could live at Elsworth Towers as Lady Elsworth – above the stares and gossip of the village.

Taking a deep breath to steady her voice, Lucinda glanced around the rose garden she loved so much. "I suppose I can take shoots of the roses I like," she said conversationally. "But you say you do have a rose garden?"

"One or two," replied Markham with a wry smile. "And, of course, we will make sure that these gardens are cared for, an arrangement you may like to supervise as well." He watched her nod as if in a dream. "Do I assume you will agree to the arrangement, Miss Stanton?" he went on.

Lucinda took a deep breath, thought for a brief moment, then turned to look at his lordship. She could be wrong, she had already been wrong about one man, but his lordship was very personable and if it meant a choice between him and George Bistow, well, there was no choice at all!

Giving her life to teaching in the little school might be an option. But even there, it would be a case of relying on charity, of scraping and saving, of mending every hole in every old stocking. And that would not take care of Milly and her family's needs. Neither would it place her beyond the censure of the villagers. And throwing herself on the mercy of unknown relatives and perhaps living a life of servitude and drudgery, would surely be a last resort. This could be a chance to solve the crisis for all concerned. And if she were to be unhappy, well, at least she would have the knowledge that she had tried to do all her mother and father would have done for Milly.

"I daresay it isn't quite the right thing to give you my reply immediately," she began slowly, "but I have spent too many sleepless nights myself to wish the same on you. If you are true to your word," she said, "I agree to the er- arrangement." She said the last with a rush of words that sounded quite stilted to her own ears. Perhaps she should have given it more thought. What would he think of her? Perhaps she should have discussed it with Milly – but, no, she could not do that. This was her decision. She had to make a choice and then Milly and Alfred had to be asked quite casually to look after Hedgeland Manor.

She began to explain this to Markham who nodded without comment. "Certainly," he replied. "They need know nothing of our arrangement beyond that we have decided to wed. No doubt there will be some talk when the word gets round, but we can ask your sister to say that we are friends of some years' standing, and have decided to wed as soon as possible for reasons that we cannot yet disclose to her."

Lucinda nodded, still feeling as if this could be a dream. But the sun was warm on her face and the bees buzzing in the wisteria were real enough.

"What do we do now?" she asked somewhat breathlessly, her confidence almost deserting her.

"The friend who gave me the news in the early hours of the morning is an apprentice in a law firm," said Markham, rising to his feet and offering Lucinda his arm as she rose. She took it tentatively. The last time she had touched a firm masculine arm, had been in fear and distress, but this arm felt strangely comforting. "I can ask him to give us legal advice," Markham was saying, "but perhaps the first thing we need to do is to draw up an agreement which we can have witnessed by your brother-in-law and also by Charlie Sutton – my friend."

"And – we can have a quiet wedding in the village church?" asked Lucinda in her most business-like voice as she strolled down the path between the roses on the arm of her future husband! "The reason I ask," she went on quickly, "is that I know the parson and his wife very well and would like them to be present."

"I have no objection," replied Markham. "I have no desire for a society wedding, even if there were time! Perhaps the best is to inform your relatives and then we can draw up the agreement and set a time for the ceremony. Unless you have any further questions?"

"No," replied Lucinda somewhat faintly, finding herself being propelled firmly back to the drawing-room.

"You don't know what this is going to mean to me," said Markham, turning to face her before they entered the house. "You are giving me back my life, and I shall keep my side of the bargain as honorably as I can!" His eyes were warm as he looked at her. His smile was sincere and genuine, thought Lucinda as she nodded, smiling in return. And he was really very handsome!

Chapter 4

Hedgeland Manor was in a tizzy! Miss Lucinda to marry Lord Elsworth! Yes, the son who went away and had now taken over the estate. Been to foreign lands and all over the world it was said. Highly thought of in the government too. Yes, it was sudden, but they had after all known each other since childhood. Grew up next door to each other, so it was obvious they must have been acquainted. Lost touch for a few years, what with the disagreement between the two neighbors in the past, but that was the past. Make a lovely couple they would.

Sarah hugged everyone in sight with tears of joy in her eyes. Of course she had known that Lady Lucinda was being secretive about something! Likely they met on some of those early morning rides! His lordship was a real gentleman, so everything would have been above board. And Lady Lucinda, for all her ways, was a true lady, and great friends with the parson and his wife. Of course she was too good for the likes of George Bistow! What a nerve the man had! Old enough to be her father and thinking he had a chance with her! In fact, she would tell him that herself if he dared call!

Millicent was in raptures! To have a permanent home for the children! To be neighbors! And for Alfred to have made such a valuable friend - why it was more than she could ever have hoped for! But she had had a good feeling about coming home - apart from the funeral, that is. But what about a dress? Couldn't the wedding be postponed for just a week?

No, replied Lucinda firmly, they had set a date and that was it. They wanted a quiet wedding with no fuss and they had set the date. There would perhaps be other celebrations later. Both she and Markham (she had practiced saying his name over and over to make it come out naturally) believed that marriage was a private contract between two people.

"I have no argument with that," the Rev. Arthur Collins replied when she repeated the statement the following day. She had gone into the village for a few yards of cream lace

WHICH MILLY HAD DEMANDED in order to 'dress up' the family wedding dress. Then she had called at the parsonage. She wanted to tell Jenny her news, although in all likelihood Lord Elsworth would have been there to obtain a special license. He had! Lucinda had worried that banns would have to be called on three consecutive Sundays, as the previous rector had insisted upon for Milly and Alfred. But Markham had simply smiled and asked her to leave it to him.

Jenny looked at her with an amazed expression when Lucinda confirmed the news she had heard, but made no comment. Instead she kissed her enthusiastically and wished her happiness, hardly able to grasp that her friend was getting married so hastily. Her husband, it was true, appeared quite at ease with the situation after the visit from Lord Markham, so perhaps she was being fanciful and old-fashioned. However, as Lucinda was leaving, she pressed her arm and whispered: "Is everything all right?" Lucinda smiled brightly, and whispered back: "Wonderful!" Jenny nodded thoughtfully. Well, time would tell, and she would be ready to support her friend if needs be. Arthur simply chuckled when she mentioned her misgivings. In his opinion it was time Lucinda married and Lord Markham was a first-class gentleman, doing a lot of good in the neighborhood. They had, after all, apparently been childhood friends.

The day after passed as a dream. Lucinda's entire wardrobe was aired, discussed and largely discarded by Milly and Sarah. Her hair was 'oiled' with a magical gleaming potion that Milly had once bought in London and that 'really worked' she was assured! The only thing it seemed to do was make her head feel cold and heavy, so Lucinda washed it out as soon as their backs were turned.

Roses were cut and sent on to the village church where Jenny would arrange them in large containers. “My sister loves roses,” Milly kept on repeating as she totally denuded the rose garden.

That afternoon, the prospective bridegroom and his friend, the honorable Charles Sutton arrived with a very legal-looking document. This time the former looked striking in a royal

blue knee-length jacket that stretched snugly over his broad shoulders and emphasized the deep blue of his eyes. It opened in front to reveal a white ruffled shirtfront, charcoal breeches and gleaming black boots. Fortunately, Lucinda had been fitting one of Milly’s London outfits - a russet gold dress in a silky material that clung to her form quite alarmingly.

Milly ushered her into the drawing room before she had time to protest. Her hair had been knotted up in a mass of curls by her sister who was trying out a style for the wedding. Markham found himself pause appreciatively, whereas the honorable Charles had to be nudged into explaining the document, his eyes wide in amazement at the woman old Mark had managed to snare at the last moment!

Lucinda listened attentively, unaware that Markham was looking decidedly more cheerful than on his previous visit. Indeed, Markham found he was pleasantly surprised. With the right clothes, there was no doubt that Lady Lucinda Stanton would not disgrace him! The old riding habit she had worn on the previous occasion had certainly not done her justice. The dress she now had on, though hardly the latest fashion, revealed enough to make him aware that his future wife had a firm slimness that was most attractive.

Lucinda appeared totally unaware of their scrutiny. “Would you like some refreshment?” she asked them in the composed manner of a well-mannered hostess. “Sarah, our housekeeper, is quite famous for her ginger and lemonade, or you may have tea or coffee.” Both men said they would try the lemonade.

While they enjoyed their refreshment, Lucinda, probably as a result of an attack of nerves, she decided later, found herself having an animated conversation with Charlie about the weather, the age of her uncle's cat and the resignation of the Duke of Newcastle from Parliament. The latter had been an acquaintance of her uncle's, who thus carefully followed any comments made about the political career of the duke in the London papers which he purchased monthly and brought home. Lucinda had had many a conversation with her uncle and thus was quite versed in the parliamentary proceedings. She realized after a while that she was probably talking too much on unladylike subjects. Lord Markham simply sat and listened, his blue gaze disconcertingly on her face, now and then giving a brief reply to a question which Charlie threw his way, but mostly watching his future wife with an unreadable expression on his face.

"Well, Pitt and Newcastle were a very unmatched pair!" Charlie was saying, shaking his head.

"Unmatched, but effective for a time," was Markham's brief comment.

"My uncle always said that the king wanted to get rid of both of them!" suggested Lucinda. She smiled at Lord Markham. "I'm sorry! I do not usually get so carried away! I must be missing the discussions I used to have with Uncle Henry."

"Don't apologize," said Markham quickly as he smiled and raised an eyebrow. "It is perfectly refreshing to hear a lady with opinions of her own regarding our government!"

"You will have to correct me if I am wrong," she said with a slight blush. "My ideas are probably quite parochial!"

"Sound good enough to me!" insisted Charlie cheerfully. "Now, if we are all ready, let's look at the documents I have drawn up." Charlie rose and gave Lucinda two neatly written documents that he had spent most of the previous afternoon preparing. They waited as she read through them silently. The language was legal in terminology, yet not difficult to understand, Lucinda discovered. She nodded now and then as she read. And then she was signing in a neat, clear hand and putting out her cool hand to seal the agreement.

When they had gone with a smile and wave and a "see you in the morning" from Lord Elsworth, Lucinda found herself in the garden. This was all happening too quickly! Was she ready to marry Lord Elsworth? It would have been far simpler had he been a brotherly type of person like Charles Sutton. They could have dealt well together, analyzing the latest news from London, laughing about the idiosyncrasies of parliamentary figures. But then, he was not as exciting as the enigmatic Lord Markham. Charlie was pleasant to look at, but did not set her heart racing as Markham did! And what did he really think of her? She was probably just a means to an end! Oh dear, she hoped she would be able to carry this off – for all of their sakes.

Well, it was too late now. The rose bushes were bare. There was the smell of raisin cakes that would be offered to any of the tenants who might call to wish her well on the morrow. And the sun was beginning to set with a rosy glow on the distant hills.

Lucinda pulled her knees up beneath her chin on the old garden seat, careful to smooth the silky gown. She lifted the old gold locket that had been her mother's and which she always wore close to her heart. Snapping it open she gazed at the cameo of the handsome laughing couple. "I'm doing it for Milly, Mother," she said softly. "And for me too, Father. I hardly know him, but I think you would have approved of him. Somehow, I will be happy! I will try to be like you! Otherwise I will run far, far away and never come back!" She swallowed the lump in her throat and sighed.

She remembered when they had first come to live at Hedgeland Manor. They had lived for a while when she was very young, in a country house a day's journey away, belonging to an aunt of her mother's. Her mother had apparently cared for the old lady, who had a great fondness for her, while her father had run the estate. When the aunt died, the property was inherited by a distant cousin, who decided to move there with his own large family. Lucinda's mother and father took away nothing more than the clothes they had, her father's small library of books (for he was a keen reader of philosophy and poetry) and a few pieces of jewelry left to Lucinda's mother by her aunt.

At that stage Uncle Henry, who had been a widower for two years and spent most of his time in London anyway, had readily invited the small family to live at Hedgelands, an arrangement that would suit them all. He and his younger brother had always been good friends.

Just a year later both Lucinda's parents had perished in the carriage accident, leaving Uncle Henry in charge of his young nieces. The poor man had been a bit out of his depth, but they had never been in want and he had even paid for a tutor for a while, an old retired schoolmaster who stayed with his sister in the village. Dear old Mr. Dove had been very patient with the two little girls.

"Basics, Sir Henry," the old schoolmaster had said. "I believe in teaching basics: reading, writing and a bit of arithmetic. Then some history and geography for the quick student. And don't let me hear that they are only girls," he had forestalled Sir Henry. "Some day they must look after themselves and hold an intelligent conversation!"

So had begun the morning lessons for the children. Lucinda remembered with nostalgia the smell of the ink, the words and figures looking like mysterious insects on the white page, and then the delight of being able to read for herself and to her younger sister. Milly did not enjoy the lessons as much as she did and would often sneak off to play her own tunes on the old harpsichord that stood in the corner of the 'schoolroom'. Mr. Dove merely shrugged and sighed and gave his full attention to Lucinda. The only time Lucinda had actually seen Mr. Dove lose composure and wipe tears of laughter from his watery old eyes, was the time that Milly composed a song of her own, the main theme being a very high soprano repetition of the words: 'We love Mr. Dove'!

Lucinda, being older, had benefited most from the three years of tutoring and had continued to read and study on her own, making use of Uncle Henry's somewhat disorganized and hardly used collection of books, mostly biographies, as well as her late father's small but fascinating collection. Some of the volumes had become firm friends on the cold winter's days when Sir Henry was away and when she found herself on her own. She would take those with her, she decided, though it was likely that Lord Markham would have a library of some proportion. The thought cheered her somewhat.

Tomorrow she was marrying a total stranger, not an old friend as people thought! And she would be beginning a new life! God give her strength and courage!

"Supper time, Lucy!" It was Milly. "We're having an early night tonight! Tomorrow is going to be a busy day!"

"Coming, Milly!" called Lucinda. She got up slowly. The garden was still heavy with the fragrance of a few spring roses, too flowered out for Milly's liking. The shadows were drawing in, the sunset an orange smear. On the horizon, the silhouette of a horseman. Joe? It looked very much like him, unless the light was deceiving. Her heart thudded uncomfortably. Anyway, what did it matter, even if it were Joe. He could do nothing to her after tomorrow! She would be safe!

There was only her family now that she had to make sure was cared for. There would be a new world of strangers - or perhaps future friends, if all went well. All that was familiar to be replaced by something new.

Exciting, yet a bit frightening. And at the back of one's mind always the nagging thought that someone had concealed part of the contents of the Elsworth will. Someone did not want the present Lord Elsworth to stay at Elsworth Towers. Time would tell.

Lucinda took a deep breath and headed for the dining salon. Sarah, in spite of her busyness had promised to make a pie with the last of the mutton.

When she entered the dining room the family were already seated and Sarah was hovering over a large unfamiliar-looking silver serving dish on which was stacked the most delectable looking roast duck surrounded by potatoes and vegetables.

"Where on earth did you get that!" exclaimed Lucinda in amazement.

"It comes from Elsworth Towers with a note from Markham saying that he is quite sure we are too busy with wedding preparations to have time to cook dinner!" said Milly airily.

"Oh, but he shouldn't have!" exclaimed Lucinda in some embarrassment. "We do have food in the house!"

"But you're engaged to the man," said Alfred as he began to carve the duck with care, "and so it is quite in order to accept his kindness." Lucinda merely shook her head and gave in with a smile. The little fingers of her niece and nephew were already reaching for a juicy bit of the roast. No doubt it had saved poor Sarah some work. The latter was cheerfully serving out the vegetables with a smile.

" 'Taint just charity, milady," she ventured as she served Lucinda. "Probably an excuse to let his man stay over."

"His man?" Lucinda frowned. "What man?"

"Kind of a footman, I reckon," replied Sarah. "Real card! Keeping us all in stitches in the kitchen!"

"Why would he want someone to stay over?" Lucinda asked, annoyed that she had not been consulted.

"Probably thinks you might escape in the night!" replied Alfred, laughing heartily at his own joke.

"Oh, nonsense, dear!" said Milly, smiling reassuringly at her sister. It wouldn't do to have her upset now and perhaps changing her mind in that willful way she had! "I asked him to send someone early in the morning to help with a few things."

Lucinda looked thoughtfully at her sister. Markham had remarked just before leaving that afternoon that he would prefer it if she stayed close to the house for the rest of the day. Was there a possibility of danger? She would have a word with the man before retiring.

The meal passed pleasantly with Lucinda finding herself laughing at the stories Alfred had to tell of their adventures in the world of artists. She suspected from Milly's amused look that some of them were highly exaggerated, but she appreciated their attempt to keep her a little distracted from the portentous decision she had made, a decision which would be solemnized the following day.

And when her two year-old niece climbed onto her lap and snuggled up, her little thumb in her mouth, her large eyes heavy with sleep, Lucinda knew that she could never have let them down or turned them out. They were part of her, and she would sacrifice a great deal to keep them safe.

"You've hardly eaten a thing, Lucy!" protested Milly as Lucinda relinquished her sleepy niece.

"I've had plenty," insisted Lucinda. "Don't forget, this will probably be my standard fare from now on!" she joked.

"You can send over the leftovers any time you like!" responded Alfred as he leaned back contentedly, his tall thin frame seemingly incapable of movement. "Need help, my love?" he half-heartedly asked, watching his wife shepherd the children to bed.

"I'll manage," she replied cheerfully. Lucinda rose quickly.

"I'll read to them, Milly," she said. "You have done more than your fair share today. Put your feet up for a while. Alice, Allen, say goodnight to your Mama and Papa." Hand in hand with Aunt Lucinda the children climbed the stairs to the next floor where the bedrooms waited.

The children dropped off to sleep within minutes. Lucinda came downstairs to join her family in the drawing room. She hesitated before entering. "If they had been childhood friends I would have known!" Milly was insisting.

"It's not really any of our business, Millicent," her husband replied. "As long as she's happy, that's the main thing."

"I keep on having this sneaking feeling that there's more to this than meets the eye! I mean, he's so devilishly handsome. He should have been married long ago!"

"They're going to make a fine couple," said Alfred. "Your sister has wonderful bone-structure."

"Spoken like a true artist!" laughed Milly. "And me - what do I have?"

"You have everything I have ever wanted," he replied softly. Lucinda smiled to herself and quietly made her way towards the kitchen. She wanted to have a few words with the so-called footman!

There was a cheerful clattering of pots and plates and an occasional whoop of laughter from Sarah's friend, Annie Moon, who had come to help with the extra work that had arisen since the funeral. She was happy with three meals a day as long as she could be flexible about her hours of work. Lucinda knew that she took most of the food home to her children and old mother.

Lord Elsworth's footman was standing up to his elbows in warm water rinsing off dinner plates when Lucinda came in. He obviously had an appreciative audience to the tale he was telling.

"Don't let me interrupt!" said Lucinda as silence fell.

"Evenin' ma'am!" said the man turning towards Lucinda and bobbing his head.

"Good evening," she replied. She noticed that he had removed his jacket and rolled up his sleeves. The muscular arms that were visible were surely not those of the standard footman!

"You are one of Lord Elsworth's footmen?" she asked politely.

"In a manner of speakin', ma'am," he replied. "I help his lordship with anything he might need me for. Me qualification is in the line of horses," he added, "mainly as in stables an' such."

"And you are here to check my stables?" Lucinda asked sweetly while Sarah smothered a chortle.

"Oh, no, ma'am," he replied somewhat embarrassed, "his lordship wanted me to lend a helping hand if needs be."

"So you're not here to spy on us?" went on Lucinda with a raised eyebrow.

"Oh, no, ma'am!" replied the man fervently. "I be here to protect the next Lady Elsworth!"

"And from what or whom do I need to be protected?" continued Lucinda aware that she was making the man uncomfortable.

"Oh there mus' be many a sad young man tonight, considerin' as yer ladyship be weddin' his lordship tomorrow!" the man replied with an impudent grin.

"All right er-"

"Biggs, Ma'am, Harold Biggs, at yer service!" He gave a short bow from the waist.

"All right, Biggs," said Lucinda with a twinkle of amusement, "thank you for your help. But perhaps it is his lordship you should be protecting from my many suitors!" she added with a laugh.

As she left she heard the inimitable Biggs chuckle and then launch into a tale of how his lordship was a real rum 'un with his fists and could throw a knife like a gipsy! My goodness, thought Lucinda, his tales would no doubt improve as the evening progressed. Gentlemen certainly did not throw knives! Well, at least, if they did, it was not common knowledge!

Milly was right, of course, Markham was a fine-looking man, a man any woman could be proud of. Perhaps it was just fate that he had not yet married. Or was there another more sinister reason? That did not bare thinking about and it would be unfair to let one's imagination run away with one. No doubt she would find out in due course in any event! But she must be positive. Raising her chin, Lucinda mounted the stairs that lead to her bedroom.

At Elsworth Towers, dusk was creeping across the graying hills. Markham was sitting in his favorite chair, sipping port and gazing into the fire. He was listening with half an ear to his friend, Charles Sutton.

"Good idea to have sent that message to old Wingate saying my father wants to see me on a family matter," he was saying, "otherwise he would wonder where I am! Can see you're used to intrigue, Mark! But why do you look so grim? You're getting yourself a fine woman, my friend! Dress her up a bit and I can't wait to see Melissa Jordan's expression!"

"You've never liked Melissa, have you, Charlie!" said Markham dryly.

"Not really. Haven't told you before. Probably can tell you now. She tried to break up Catherine and me. Told Cathy I was the kind who preferred men's company only!"

"Why would she have said a thing like that?" said Markham with a frown.

"I told Cathy she was probably jealous we were so happy. That was when your father died and you decided to come to Elsworth Towers. Reckon she was upset about that too. She told everyone she would persuade you to stay in London and forget about the boring countryside when you married her! When you didn't ask her, she was off on the Grand Tour!"

"Indeed!" said Markham with a wry smile. "I must have misread the signals, or else my mind was too occupied with my plans for the Towers at that stage." As he gazed into the dancing flames he could see the golden tresses and turquoise eyes of the rather lovely Melissa Jordan, London's darling for at least two seasons, until the old tabbies had discovered that bit of scandal about her! Seems she had a secret liaison with the Earl of Chester, a man old enough to be her father. That was but a rumor until she appeared at a ball wearing a ruby as big as a bird's egg, set in the Chester style and recognized by someone as being part of a set belonging to the Countess who was away visiting her sister in Scotland at the time. Melissa simply laughed, letting it be known that it was a gift from a friend. She continued to sport the ruby, but not, it was noted, after the Countess returned! Since then the Earl had apparently been taken ill and was living at one of his country homes.

Markham, finding himself often in need of a companion at official functions or social gatherings, had been on the point of testing the waters there, his own reputation not being an issue, when his father became very ill. Ah well, he could live without Melissa Jordan. His affections had never actually become engaged in that direction. He wondered what her reaction would be to his marriage! And his other friends as well!

"Do you know a good seamstress?" he asked suddenly.

"Catherine will," replied Charlie. "You mean for Lucinda?"

"Most definitely!" replied Markham. "I have a feeling that her wardrobe is rather limited. Damn uncle probably kept them on a shoestring while he gambled his money away!"

"She's a striking woman, even now!" said Charles enthusiastically.

"You think so?" murmured Markham with a short sigh. "She certainly seems to be composed, perhaps too composed and to know her own mind given the circumstances in which she finds herself! Hope she has a bit more warmth in her than appears on the surface!"

"Of course she has!" exclaimed Charlie. "Didn't you see her with the children? They adore her! And anyway, since when has there been a woman born who has not melted at the feet of Markham Elsworth!"

"Hmm," responded Markham. "Ah well, she will be my wife. That's all that matters for the present."

Chapter 5

Lucinda did not expect to sleep well. She lay deep in thought for a while after sipping the hot toddy Milly had brought her. Milly would not tell her what was in it, just that it was herbal and would help her relax.

When she opened her eyes it was to the rattle of her teacup as Sarah brought in the tea and the unfamiliar sound of hot water being poured into the bathtub so early in the morning.

"Do I have to get up yet?" she murmured sleepily.

"Wedding's set for eleven. We don't want to have to rush, milady," said Sarah firmly. "You will want your bath and Miss Milly will want to do your hair. Then it's breakfast to be got and before we know it, the carriage will be at the door!"

"All right, dear Sarah! Brides are allowed to be a little late though!"

'Never agreed with that meself! Seems like bad manners to me!" said Sarah firmly. She assisted Lucinda into the bath as if she were an invalid and then proceeded to scrub her back with soap, as she had done when Lucinda was a child. Milly entered the room breezily and added rose essence to the rinsing water. Then a fluffy white towel that Lucinda had never seen before was wrapped around her. She was not allowed to protest as both Sarah and Milly rubbed sweet-smelling oil on her limbs. "I am not an Eastern princess!" she protested, but Milly merely grinned as she helped her into fresh underwear and a robe, took her off to the room belonging to their late mother and sat her down to begin working on her hair.

Lucinda cast a quick glance at the wedding dress hanging in front of the old wardrobe. Milly certainly had a talent with the needle. The old cream silk dress, which Milly herself had worn on her wedding day had needed only a slight alteration in length. Milly had added a lacy frill which was balanced by row upon row of lace of the same shade caught in loops by the palest lemon rose-buds. These had been skillfully crafted from strips of a diaphanous scarf that Milly declared had made her look very uninteresting and pale. Lemon was not her color, but would look delightful on Lucinda. The short train of the dress was draped over a chair over which hung also a veil, with a small pearly coronet that had belonged to their mother. Here and there on the skirt of the dress a pearl gleamed. Milly had found the remnants of an old necklace that had never been restrung and had cheerfully put it to use. Lucinda smiled. She might not be in the height of fashion, but she would look like a real bride after all!

"Thank you, Milly," she said as she smiled at her sister's reflection in the mirror. "I don't know what I would have done without you!"

"Nonsense!" said Milly through a mouthful of hairpins. "You have always taken the greatest care of me. Now it is my turn to do just a little in return!"

"Oh, Milly!" exclaimed Lucinda, her eyes misting. "You reminded me so much of Mama just then! Do you think she can see us now?"

"Maybe," said Milly with a short sigh and a shrug of her shoulders. "Do you still remember her, Lucy? I don't remember her at all."

"You were too young," said Lucinda slowly. They had had this conversation a number of times. "But you are very much like her – full of fun, artistic and a wonderful mother!"

"And so will you be one day!" declared Milly with a quick smile as she noticed Lucinda's expression. She carefully pinned a stray curl. "And you are far prettier than I am and clever as well! And just let Markham say anything to the contrary! He will have me to deal with!"

"Oh, Milly!" laughed Lucinda as Milly put on her sternest expression while her eyes twinkled.

AS IT TURNED OUT, THE bridal party arrived in good time, much to the relief of both the groom and his groomsman. Markham had been uneasy until he saw his bride arrive. Charles sensed his friend's agitation and tried to keep him distracted until he realized that Markham was not listening to a word he said. But it was understandable, he supposed, so much hinged on his being married that very day!

The Elsworth carriage drew up outside the village church exactly on the hour. Alfred alighted, followed by his wife, Millicent, who was quite a sight for sore eyes, as one of the curious villagers put it, in a pale blue silky dress with a small hat with feathers in the same color perched on her golden curls.

Then followed the bride herself in a cream, lace-trimmed dress with a full skirt that had been her own late mother's wedding dress, veil kept in place by a shiny pearl coronet and clutching a posy of pale yellow flowers which matched those on the skirt of the dress, though of course the former were real! She was followed by Sarah Greenley, housekeeper, wearing her Sunday best, but having added a deep pink feather to her usual black hat! Well, one could not blame her for being proud on this day, what with both young ladies being safely married! Then there were the two little ones both dressed in blue like their mother, spick and span and for once as good as gold.

Miss Lucinda was led into the church by her brother-in-law and the organ music began - played of course by the parson's own wife.

Lucinda found her feet moving automatically and might have stumbled had it not been for Alfred's arm onto which she held as to a lifeline. The music stopped and there she was beside Lord Markham Elsworth, who was looking quite resplendent in a grey pin-striped morning coat with a white embroidered shirtfront, grey close-fitting pantaloons and gleaming black boots. Beside him was Charles Sutton in a dark grey coat, smiling as if it were the happiest day of his life!

Lucinda felt Alfred prize her fingers from his arm and give her a reassuring wink as Lord Markham took her hand. She stole a quick glance at him through her veil. His face was impassive, but she sensed the tension in the clasp of his hand. Did he perhaps feel as nervous as she did? The thought cheered her for a moment, and as if he read her thoughts, he glanced down at her, his lips moved in the ghost of a smile and he squeezed her hand.

Then they were both caught up in the unreality of hearing themselves repeat vows to "love and cherish, to honor ... for better or for worse, until death did them part!" The church was quiet and their voices seemed to hang in the air as they followed the sonorous tones of the parson. There was a gentle sniffling sound which Lucinda knew could only emanate from Sarah and for a moment her own eyes misted. Sarah was the closest she had known to a mother.

But this was no time for reflection! Markham was waiting for her to extend her left hand. Milly took the posy with alacrity and Lucinda found herself staring down at a magnificent emerald encircled by diamonds. The ring glided smoothly onto her ring finger and she looked up to see an amused smile transform Markham's inscrutable expression. The ring fitted perfectly!

Then Charles was handing her a heavy gold signet ring to slip onto Markham's ring finger. The deed was done! Milly lifted her veil and arranged it neatly. Markham stooped to plant a gentle kiss on her lips. Hugs and congratulations were passed around.

"You look beautiful, Lucy!" whispered Jenny. "And I want you to be very happy!" Then she turned to Markham. "She is one of the finest people I know - be good to her!"

"That is my every intention!" replied his lordship with a most charming smile, which dispelled any reservations Jenny might have had about the suitability of the alliance!

"Jolly good show!" Charles was saying to Lucinda. "Splendid flowers!"

"Yes," murmured Lucinda, only then noticing the roses that spilled in profusion from numerous large vases. "Thank you, Jenny," she said to her friend who was still hovering close by.

"Oh, it was nothing!" exclaimed Jenny, still a little concerned though at her friend's paleness.

"You were both wonderful!" Millicent was saying. "Not a stammer or a stutter! Not like me - I kept on forgetting what to say next!" Lucinda joined in the laughter, her own eyes twinkling as she recalled her sister's wedding. Both Milly and Alfred had been so nervous!

"Time to play the wedding march, my dear," said the Rev. Collins to his wife, Jenny, and the latter quickly slipped in behind the little pedal organ and Arthur Collins grouped the wedding party. Markham had retained hold of Lucinda's hand and now he slipped it firmly into the crook of his arm. He gave her a reassuring wink and the bridal party left the cool little rose-scented church.

To Lucinda's surprise, and she could sense from his brief hesitation that Markham was also somewhat taken aback, most of the village seemed grouped outside and in festive mood. Calls of "Well done to ye both!" and "Happy days to ye!" were mingled with a scattered round of applause. Lucinda felt quite touched by the gesture of goodwill. A few young children whom she recognized as scholars from the little school near the church, ran forward with a basket of rose petals which they scattered in the path of the bridal couple. Probably Jenny's doing!

Lucinda looked up to smile at Markham. She knew every one of these villagers. They liked nothing better than a bit of gossip in their somewhat routine existence. She would play the part of the happy bride. She wanted no speculation and no unpleasant gossip!

Markham had a relaxed smile on his handsome face, but Lucinda could sense the tension in the muscle of the arm she was holding onto. Just a few more paces to the waiting carriage.

Then a cackle and a loud call from one of the groups: "Why such a hasty weddin' milady? Be ye carryin' 'is Lordship's bairn?" There was a sudden hush and an intake of breath. The smile froze on Markham's face.

Lucinda took a deep breath, then she called on every ounce of composure she had and smiled as she turned towards the direction of the voice: "Not yet, old Nell, not yet!" she said in an exaggerated conspiratorial stage whisper. There was a hoot of laughter from a group nearest to them and then chuckles and another scattered round of applause. Everyone knew old Nell well enough to know that she had no inhibitions, but meant no harm! What a nerve to tease Miss Lucinda! Luckily she could give as good as she got!

Markham smiled down at her with an amused twinkle in his eyes and she deliberately lifted a hand to touch his cheek. She saw a flicker of admiration in his eyes as he acknowledged her strategy.

He was about to hand her into the carriage when she sensed someone had stepped forward and was standing a little too close to her. Her eyes flew wide for a moment, and she clutched onto Markham's arm as dizziness assailed her. It was Joe Thackeray, his tanned face looking down at her above a spotless white shirt and checked waistcoat. He was standing too close to her but she stood her ground.

"Congratulations, Lucinda," he said in clipped tones, almost daring her to reprove him for the use of her name and for his tone of familiarity. His eyes glittered into her own and then he let his gaze travel down to the curve of her breast. Anger swept through her then and her mind which had frozen, began to function rationally once again.

"Thank you," Lucinda found herself replying coldly.

"You needn't have done this, Lucinda!" he said almost fiercely. "Though this one beats old Bistow in looks!"

"Thackeray, is it?" interrupted Markham smoothly. "Would you mind stepping back? My wife would like to throw the traditional posy of flowers!" Leaning on Markham's arm, Lucinda stepped onto the second step of the carriage, her head now on a level with Markham's. Her lips were slightly parted and her cheeks, she knew, were flushed. She closed her eyes and flung the posy into a group of girls who jumped and shrieked with delight.

Luckily, everyone's attention was diverted by the posy-throwing. Only Lucinda and Markham heard the unkind tone in Joe's voice as he said quite clearly to her: "So ye be happy with the child, then?" Lucinda had no idea what he was referring to, but with every intent to annoy Joe Thackeray further, she laughed merrily and put Markham's hand to her lips.

Then with a wave of her hand on which glittered the Elsworth emerald, she slipped into the carriage. Markham followed her, the door was closed by an ever-vigilant Biggs, and she let out a trembling sigh of relief and blinked back tears as she sank back against the plush red cushions.

She glanced sideways at Markham who was regarding her calmly. "I'm sorry -" she began, "for the villagers all being there, and I think Joe Thackeray must have been tipsy to act and speak so strangely!"

"I suppose you didn't organize the reception - and you can't blame them," he replied. "They've known you a long time, no doubt."

"Yes," said Lucinda. "They all turned out for Milly's wedding too. I should have expected it!" She knew she was talking too rapidly, but she had to speak to stop her teeth from chattering.

"What is your relationship with Thackeray?" Markham asked suddenly.

"I know his mother quite well," Lucinda replied a little too quickly, trying to keep her voice as steady as possible, but not succeeding too well, and avoiding his eye.

"It will not be my policy to choose your friends, Lucinda," Markham said rather stiffly, "but there is something very arrogant about that fellow. He has always refused to attend any of the meetings I have called."

"He is that!" agreed Lucinda quickly. "And he's no friend of mine!" Lucinda knew her face was flushed.

Fortunately, just then another larger carriage overtook them and both Lucinda and Markham found themselves laughing and waving. It was the older crested Elsworth carriage containing a grinning, waving Charles and the rest of Lucinda's family!

"I have invited them for a celebration tea," explained Markham. "I suppose I should have checked with you first -"

"Oh no, that's wonderful!" insisted Lucinda. At least she would have Milly and Sarah with her for the first few hours in her new home, a home she had yet to enter! And there would be no more talk about Joe!

Just then they crested a small hill and to Lucinda's puzzlement, the horses came to a standstill. Markham opened the door and extended his hand to Lucinda. "I asked Kidson to stop when we got here," he explained. Lucinda alighted from the carriage, her train looped over one arm, and allowed Markham to lead her to the other side of the carriage.

"Your new home!" he said with a sweep of his arm. Lucinda looked down at the magnificent scene. There was Elsworth Towers – a great pile of pink granite with its bay windows, balconies, chimneys and towers. It had been so named because each time a new wing was added, it had become traditional to add a tower as well. Four towers now caught the morning sunshine, which glistened on the small lake and on the riot of color which was the gardens and the expanse of lawns. Stately pillars rose from the green lawns and peeped out from the shrubs and trees that had been planted to grace them. An avenue of a hundred year-old oak trees, now fresh with a batch of new green leaves, lined the path they would soon be following.

Markham placed his left arm lightly round her waist and with his right arm, pointed as he spoke. "That is the South Wing where the main gardens are. My grandfather built that and my mother and father always occupied it. On the other side, the North Wing, the oldest section, which contains the kitchens, laundry, servants' rooms and so on. The side we can't see, the East Wing, has a suite of rooms that my step-mamma redecorated and enjoyed, and then, of course, the West Wing, which consists of the entrance hall, guest-rooms, the ballroom and a few drawing-rooms."

"It's beautiful!" said Lucinda sincerely, aware of the pride in her husband's voice.

"Different to what you remember?" asked Markham.

"Oh, yes!" said Lucinda. "I probably saw it last a dozen years ago. It was winter at the time and I thought the towers with their heavy covering of snow looked rather forbidding and mysterious! My uncle and your father had a disagreement about tenants, I think, so we did not socialize with your family."

Markham turned to look at her. His blue gaze was serious as he took her hands in his. "That is history, fortunately!" said Markham evenly. "I want you to be happy here, Lucinda. I know our marriage is a very hasty and unusual one, but I am very grateful to you that I do not have to leave all this. You have made that possible."

"I am just grateful that my family is secure," said Lucinda with a suggestion of tears in her large green eyes. Markham gazed down at her for a moment, his eyes travelling to her soft lips which held the suspicion of a tremble as she spoke.

Then he nodded. "I want us to be open and honest with each other. It may be difficult at times, but we need to begin afresh and together!"

"Yes," agreed Lucinda, wondering somewhat at his serious expression. Then Markham took a deep breath, gave her a slight hug and smiled.

"Come, we had better not keep our guests waiting too long!" he said, helping her into the carriage once again.

They were just about to set off on the last leg of their short journey, when there was a sharp, shrill whistle. Before Kidson had a chance to get the horses moving, a rider arrived, dust swirling. He leaped off a tall black horse and immediately rushed over to Markham's side of the carriage.

"What is it, Biggs?" asked Markham fairly calmly in the face of such haste. He opened his carriage door and Biggs, covered in dust and perspiring somewhat gave a short bow in the direction of Lucinda.

"Milady, Milord," he said a bit breathlessly. "I have come to warn you!"

"Go on," said Markham, while Kidson waited patiently, out of earshot, as there was a partition between him and the passengers.

"Lady Amelia and son Lawrence have arrived! Have rooms at the Royal Arms," said Biggs grimly. He glanced at Markham's unimpressed expression and then took a deep breath. "They have four very able-bodied men with them (no doubt hired in London) and their groom secretly told one of our grooms, on pain of death, that they were planning to kidnap your bride and keep you apart until tomorrow! Something about legal deadlines!"

"They probably want to keep us apart and then annul our marriage tomorrow. That was the deadline." said Lord Markham, looking at Lucinda's puzzled expression.

"But we are married!" she exclaimed. She noticed Biggs move away slightly.

"True," replied Lord Markham, looking at her carefully, "but an annulment can be made if - if the marriage has not been consummated."

"Of course!" Lucinda replied swiftly, feeling a bit foolish at her reasoning. "Well, then - we don't go back to Elsworth until tomorrow!" she replied firmly,

"Of course!" nodded Markham with a slightly admiring twinkle in his eyes. "Biggs - any suggestions?"

"Um - there is the old Elmsford Arms, milord, but likely that's the first place they'll look for ye." Lord Markham nodded.

Lord Markham took a deep breath and frowned slightly. Suddenly Biggs' face lit up. "Me sister's cottage! She be visiting our grandma until end of month!"

"And she wouldn't mind?" asked Lucinda a bit nervously.

"Not at all, Your Ladyship!" replied Biggs proudly. "She keeps a neat little home and would welcome ye with open arms!"

"Where is the cottage?" asked Lord Markham.

"At the edge of New Forest!" replied Biggs. "But twenty minutes walk away near the river."

"But we can't take the carriage there, can we?" asked Lord Markham. "Anyone searching will see it soon enough!"

"My suggestion, Sir," replied Biggs with folded arms, which confirmed to Lucinda that these two men had somehow been together in the military as she suspected, "is that Mr. Kidson drives the carriage to the inn close by. I'll help hide it well and then we fetch ye in the morning to return to Elsworth! That is, if Lady Elsworth agrees to a short walk to me sister's cottage!"

"I find that acceptable," replied Lucinda with a grateful smile, which immediately brought an answering grin from Biggs. This lady was just what his lordship needed!

Without further ado, Biggs stood back for his lordship to alight. Markham quickly went round to Lucinda's carriage door and helped her out. She had carefully removed her veil and coronet and pushed them under the seat out of sight. She was indeed rather pleased that her fairly worn shoes which had been painted gold by her sister, were comfortable to walk in.

Lord Markham quickly walked over to the astonished Kidson to explain the new arrangement, but he nodded enthusiastically. Biggs tied the black stallion to the back of the carriage and Kidson set off slowly in the direction of the inn.

Biggs gave a brief nod and bow once again and Markham took Lucinda's hand. They crossed the road and began to follow a narrow pathway through tall grass and bushes. Lucinda had no fear of a misstep, as Markham held her hand firmly and even took her arm on occasions. Within a few minutes, she could hear the gurgling sound of the river. She gathered her skirts as they passed bushes which threatened to cover the pathway.

Within ten minutes or so, they had reached a small clearing near a waterfall. About fifty yards away stood a neat cottage set in a well-kept garden. Gibbs marched up the garden path, slid his hand under a stone near the door and then ushered them into the cottage. The curtains were drawn and thus the light was much dimmer. He was about to remedy that, when Lord Markham put up his hand.

"Let's leave it look as if it is unoccupied, Biggs," he said calmly. "You may be assured that we will reimburse your sister for her help -"

"Oh, my lord, she will be thrilled to have helped in such an escapade! She is always ready for a lark!" he exclaimed, and then wondered if perhaps that was the correct term to have used.

Lord Markham laughed as did Lady Lucinda, and he felt better. Then Biggs paused. "I forgot about what ye will eat!" He quickly entered the kitchen. On a counter was a bright red tin. He opened it. "Looks like me sister, Jane's, home-made biscuits!"

He shook his head dismally until Lucinda said in a cheerful voice: "There is plenty of fruit in the bowl on the table! Biscuits and fruit will be a fine wedding repast!" They all joined her laughter.

"And I have found a bottle of cherry wine!" grinned his lordship, who had looked in another cupboard. "We shall exchange that later with Jane for champagne!"

Meanwhile Biggs had ducked into a bedroom nearby. He came out and smiled. "Plenty warm blankets for ye there, seeing as ye won't be able to use the stove or fire-place!"

"Thank you, Biggs!" replied Lucinda cheerfully again.

"And milady, I truly mean this. If ye want to use any article of clothing belonging to Jane, 'twould be her greatest honor! I think ye be about of the same stature," he added.

"Come now, Biggs, let's not discuss my wife's stature!" said Markham with a twinkling grin.

"My apologies, Sir!" replied the rather impudent Biggs with his best salute. "I'll be going now! I'll fetch ye, shall we say at about nine o'clock tomorrow morning? Ye should be ready for a hearty Elsworth breakfast by then!"

"Thank you, Biggs!" replied Markham, his face now intently serious. "I really owe you for this!"

" Not after ye saved me life three times, Sir!" grinned Biggs. He bowed briefly to Lucinda, put the key on the inside of the door, and indicated to Markham that he lock it immediately. Lord Markham strode swiftly over to Briggs and said a word or two which Lucinda could hear included discreet messages to her sister and to Charles, and then Biggs was gone - as silently as a breeze.

Lord Markham then proceeded to fetch the cherry wine from the kitchen, found two suitable glasses and poured half a glass each. He handed one to Lucinda who was sitting on the couch wide-eyed, trying hard to believe that this was real.

Markham grinned in appreciation. "Strange adventure we're having," he said as a giggle escaped her lips. Then he took the glass from her and put it down on the small coffee table in front of them, beside his own. He took her left hand in his own and put the beautiful emerald ring to his lips. "I'd like to say this, my lovely Lucy: today we made vows together in that little church. I am someone who has always believed that one should keep one's word under all circumstances. So - I promise again that I shall love you and cherish you (as I believe that is a choice) and I shall never ever leave you for anyone else! You have virtually sacrificed your future for me and for your family, and I respect that beyond words!"

Lucinda felt tears come to her eyes and her lips trembled a little as she replied: "I could never ask for anything more! I can already see in you a man I can admire and love and cherish as well!"

Markham cupped her face in his hands and gave her a gentle kiss on the lips. Lucinda gave a light sigh. This was so beautiful and so different from the demanding kisses of some men! Then she accepted the glass he handed to her, they clinked glasses and laughingly toasted one another!

A moment later, Markham stood up. He took Lucinda's hand and pulled her to her feet. "Come, wife," he said with the delightful twinkle she often noticed in his eyes, "we have an appointment to keep!"

With that, he led her quickly, yet gently, to the adjoining bedroom, where the blankets had already been turned back.

Chapter 6

The night was dark and chilly, but both Lucinda and Markham were warm and cozy as they slept. As the sun began to rise, Lucinda opened her eyes, for a moment not quite sure where she was. Then she turned towards the movement on the other side of the bed. Her husband (yes, indeed, her very own husband) was carefully pulling on his boots.

"Good morning, Lady Elsworth!" he said with a broad smile. "I trust you enjoyed the night as much as I did!"

"Oh yes, my Lord!" replied Lucinda with an answering and rather pert smile. "But pray, what is our program for today?"

"Unfortunately, as soon as Biggs arrives, we must show ourselves at Elsworth Estate! I cannot offer to run you a warm bath! I took a cold one myself and it reminded me of my early days in the military!" Lord Markham raised his eyebrows as he asked: "Are you going to follow suit?"

"Of course!" replied Lucinda firmly as she swung her naked legs out of the bed, grabbed the sheet to wrap around herself against the chill and taking a deep, dramatic breath, headed for the small bathroom opposite.

With more bravado than delight, she splashed water over herself and soaped herself thoroughly with the cake of vanilla-scented soap that obviously belonged to Jane. Then she had no option but to dry herself with the sheet before heading back to the bedroom where her clothes were.

She also had no option but to slip into her family wedding dress which could have done with a bit of ironing. She slipped on her shoes, clasped the pearl necklace she had been wearing around her neck and bravely advanced to the kitchen where Markham was slicing fruit on a board. He had already provided enough for an early snack and washed his hands in a bowl of cold water and dried them thoroughly.

"My next step, I know, is to fasten all those little buttons down your back!" he said with a grin.

"Indeed!" replied Lucinda as she turned her back towards him. "But what can I do about my hair? I am sure it is decidedly unacceptable!"

"Hmm," murmured Markham as he walked off to the main bedroom. He returned with a brush. He looked at her critically. "All I can do to help is to remove the pins from your hair and then brush it to its shining glory as it hangs onto your shoulders!"

Lucinda knew that her hair usually fell quite naturally into loose curls if let down. "Go ahead, husband!" she teased. "You are a man of many talents, it seems!"

"I can assure you that you don't know the half of them yet!" laughed Markham as she sat on a straight-backed chair, and humming a cheerful tune, he proceeded to pretend he was indeed her maid! Then he paused and brushed her hair gently. "You have beautiful hair, Lucy!" he said earnestly. "As far as I'm concerned, you can always wear it down! We won't give a hoot what our guests say!"

Lucinda laughed, took the brush and pins from him and went to the main bedroom for a quick look in the small mirror at the style he liked. Her hair was certainly shining this morning. Could it be the oil that her sister had insisted on applying? Her dress was also passable and the pearls blinked encouragingly at her.

Markham had drawn up another straight-backed chair to the little dining table. He had also poured a bit more cherry wine into the glasses. "I think we had better fortify ourselves!" he said with a grimace. "I assure you I do not drink wine for breakfast, but it should taste good with this fruit. And I must warn you that my relatives will have some rather unkind comments to make!"

"I shall pretend I am acting in a play and will be as kind as I can!" said Lucinda with a grin. "Nothing they say can change who we are now!"

"Well said, my dear wife!" replied Markham, raising his glass to her. Then she noticed that he glanced at her quickly and then glanced away as if making a decision. He took a deep breath and then said: "There is just one thing you don't yet know about me, which I would like to share with you myself."

Lucinda paused, but stared at him calmly. "Go on," she said.

Markham cleared his throat. "As I was leaving India a year ago, just as I was about to step on board ship, a rather strange-looking Indian woman came up to me and passed me something. Biggs was next to me, so he stepped in front of me. He could speak some of the dialect and the woman soon hurried away. When he turned around, I had the shock of my life, because he was holding a bundle in his arm. It was a tiny baby, which the woman had forced on him, saying that it was my child! She said she had saved it from drowning!"

"And then -?" went on Lucinda, more curious than shocked.

Biggs and I hurried up to my cabin. It was indeed a baby - a girl. She started to make crying sounds, so Biggs took the bottle that was wrapped with her and put it in her mouth. She had a slightly darker complexion than mine, but when she opened her little eyes, they were the exact blue color of mine." Lord Markham had now put his head in his hands. Lucinda stretched out her hand to touch his arm gently.

"I had not had any intimacies with any of the Indian ladies. In fact, it would have been frowned upon! But then I remembered the trip to the hills. We were accompanied by a chaperone and some young women. One of them was the daughter of my host. We rested at midday, and the girls picked flowers. One of them had some kind of musical instrument and they began to dance. It was some kind of ceremony to their gods. They finished their dance and then fed us on traditional food as well as some kind of drink in a large cup. I thought I felt my head spin after that. I felt a bit dizzy and tried to get up. When I eventually focused and opened my eyes properly, everyone was gone! Everyone, except the daughter of my host, who was lying next to me. I was horrified and apologetic, but she just gathered up her clothes and laughed merrily. Then she, too, was gone! Somehow, Biggs managed to track me down!"

Lord Markham had grown quite pale as he went on, now taking Lucinda's hand in his own. "The young lady in question had been promised to someone, and had probably wanted a last fling! They had planned to drown the child at birth. One old relative had rescued the little one and journeyed to the harbor. Biggs, in his usual fashion, took over! He has twin sons of his own who are with his wife in one of our cottages. He organized food from the galley for his 'adopted' daughter as he told the cook and we managed to bring her back to Elsworth without anyone any the wiser. (I have since, of course, legally adopted her myself.) My old butler, Smithson, immediately fetched his retired sister to occupy the South Wing, placed a constant guard at the top of the stairs and allowed me to complete my reports in London."

"Where is the little one now?" asked Lucinda anxiously, imagining an unhappy baby.

"Little Susan (as I decided to call her) is still at Elsworth - now a year old." He paused. "I'm sorry, Lucinda, I suppose I should have told you this earlier." He gripped her hand harder as he looked at her face, trying to read her expression.

"My dear Markham," Lucinda said with tears in her eyes, "I could never turn a child away! I missed my mother too much to want to do that to any other child!"

Lord Markham went on his knees beside her and rested his head on her lap. Lucinda stroked his hair as he said: "I don't deserve you, you know that! I selfishly thought that you may reject my proposal and all would be lost! That is why I waited until now to tell you!" There were tears on his cheeks as he raised his head. Lucinda wiped his cheeks with her hands and bent down to kiss him in a heart-stopping manner.

Just at that moment there was a light knock on the door. Lord Markham rose to his feet, wiped his eyes with his handkerchief, and looking at his watch, nodded. It was five minutes to nine.

He opened the door to a smiling Biggs, who, although he could see he may have knocked at an inopportune time, bowed respectfully. "Good morning, milady, milord! The carriage awaits ye as soon as ye are ready! "

To Lucinda and Markham's surprise, there was an older woman behind him, with clothes draped over her arms.

"Emily!" exclaimed Markham as he stepped forward impulsively to give the old lady a hug. Then he turned to Lucinda: "My love, this is my late mother's very own personal maid! Where have you come from, Emily! And why are you here?"

"Always so full of questions he was, even as a child," replied the delighted Emily as she winked at Lucinda. "I have brought you both a change of clothing! Can't have the staff and all have rumors flying around!" She was holding an emerald green dress over one arm, which Lucinda recognized as one her sister had passed on to her. Over the other arm, was a deep green jacket that belonged to Markham and the rest of an outfit to match!

"That is so thoughtful of you!" said Lucinda warmly as she guided the older lady inside, relieving her of her burdens. "Here we are, Mark!" she said with a grin. Biggs can help you while I spend a short while with Emily!"

Biggs grinned affably and then he added with a sly grin as he looked at Lord Markham: "They searched for both of ye last night! A couple of the lads and I sorted them out at the inn! Those four rascals will not return here again, if I may say so! And all is well on the Estate - though the visitors we had rather not see, have not yet left!"

"Thank you, Biggs!" replied Lord Markham. "That must have been quite a spectacle!"

"You are a capable man, Biggs, with both young and old!" added Lucinda with a smile. Biggs knew then that Lord Markham must have told her about the baby! He grinned and bowed again.

Lucinda led the way to the main bedroom, where Emily proudly helped her dress in the emerald green dress that matched her eyes to perfection! It had a heart-shaped neckline and slightly puffed sleeves that ended just above her elbows. The skirt was fairly full with some glittering flounces in gold ribbon.

Lucinda looked at herself in the mirror and smiled. "I am so grateful to you, dearest Emily!"

"It is my greatest pleasure to see Lord Markham married to a fine, beautiful, kind lady! Biggs has told me a lot about you!" she added, as she began to brush Lucinda's hair and deftly threaded a few gold ribbons that she had obviously removed from an inconspicuous place on the skirt of the dress. Her auburn hair still hung to her shoulders, but was now neater and more groomed. Then, Emily put her hand in her pocket and took out a beautiful delicate gold necklace.

Lucinda's eyes widened as Emily explained with a smile: "Biggs got this from Smithson who knew where some of the jewelry belonging to Lord Markham's mother was stored! Then, to match, there are these earrings!" Lucinda gasped as the delicate, gold earrings that ended in an emerald stone, were inserted in her ears.

Emily carefully folded the wedding dress and placed the pearls that Lucinda had been wearing in a little purse. "I shall return all this to your sister, milady!" she said with a smile. Then she opened another container and gently brushed Lucinda's cheeks with a very light powder that highlighted her cheekbones. This was followed by a glossy substance for her lips. A spray of perfume behind each ear completed the process.

"That sister of mine!" exclaimed Lucinda. "Now I know what she was up to in Paris!" Emily laughed and clapped her hands in delight.

"Even if I say so myself, milady, you will charm everyone you speak to today!" chuckled Emily.

"I appreciate the confidence you have given me, dearest Emily! I think I may need it! And I shall definitely keep in touch with you!" Lucinda twirled around and laughingly joined the gentlemen.

"Wow!" exclaimed Biggs with mock humor. "Then he bowed to Lucinda politely and grinned at Markham in mock apology,

"I shall excuse you this time, Corporal," replied Lord Markham with a grin, "as I happen to echo your sentiments. You look beautiful, my love!" With that he gave Emily a grateful smile and proceeded to lead Lucinda out to the carriage which was waiting.

"Aren't you coming with us, Emily?" queried Markham.

"Thank you, kindly, but no!" replied the older lady. "This is my niece's house, so I plan to prepare for her return. That gentleman of yours is my nephew!"

Lord Markham grinned and shook his head. "Small world!" he said.

Within ten minutes, both Lucinda and Markham found themselves being bowled along in the carriage that had taken them to the church - but now on their way home!

Chapter 7

When they drew up at the wide flight of marble steps which led up to a pillared portico, Markham helped his new bride alight.

"I'm sorry, more scrutiny!" he muttered as he indicated the line of curious servants whom Smithson had lined up according to rank. "Old Smithson's idea, no doubt!"

"That's all right," replied Lucinda, lifting her chin and smiling at the anxious Smithson. One thing she did know was how to run a household! None of them would fault her, she promised herself. "You must be Smithson?" she said addressing the old man who bowed courteously.

"I am indeed, milady," replied the old man proudly. "Milord?" He turned to Lord Markham who was regarding the scene with wry amusement.

"Yes, what is it, Smithson?" he drawled with a raised eyebrow. Lucinda glanced at him and quickly hid the twinkle in her eye.

"Would you please allow me to introduce the staff to their new mistress?"

"By all means, Smithson," replied Markham patiently. "I should be most grateful if you would!"

The old man bowed once more, then with extreme correctness and firm steps, led the way towards the waiting staff.

Lucinda, trying to be as elegant as she could, stopped before each one, smiled, inclined her head as they bowed or dropped a curtsey and tried to have a word for each. The row began with Mrs. Potters, the housekeeper, who was also at present the cook. Then there were her two assistants, two middle-aged women named Ada and Elva who looked very much alike and were indeed twin sisters, confirmed Smithson, giving them a frown as they both giggled self-consciously. Next was a dark-haired young woman, probably in her late teens, who looked at Lucinda somewhat curiously before she quickly dropped her eyes and curtsied. She was a lady's-maid-in-training declared Smithson. Two footmen bowed hastily and lastly, the old gardener, John Tonkins, and his two assistants, acknowledged their new mistress.

"Thank you, Smithson," Lucinda said clearly. "I am sure Mrs. Potters will explain your duties to me at her earliest convenience," she added addressing the group, "and I shall be conferring with you, Mr. Tonkins, in the very near future." Mrs. Potters nodded briefly and from the gleam in her eye, Lucinda knew she had said the right thing. It was always wise to have the housekeeper on your side! Tonkins showed his uneven yellow teeth in a friendly smile. They'd said this one was keen on gardens!

Well, thought Markham Elsworth wryly: one advantage of marrying someone who had been a housekeeper, she at least knew how to handle servants! He put out his hand and she took his with a slight nod and a smile and sailed up the steps, her head held high, her silken dress swishing regally behind her. The servants began to whisper and even Mrs. Potters nodded her head slightly as she caught the eye of her old friend, Tonkins, the head gardener. The new mistress had certainly made a better impression than the last one! Lady Amelia had always walked past them as if they were pieces of furniture or shrubs in the garden.

At the top of the steps was a wide landing. Here they were met by the Honorable Charles and Lucinda's family with cries of: "Here they are!" Charles blocked the doorway with a mischievous grin on his face. To both Markham and Lucinda's consternation, they noticed a large bruise over one of his eyebrows, but he shook his head at Markham before he could comment.

"Got to carry your bride over the threshold, Mark, old lad!" he declared. "Not quite the thing to let her come inside on her own steam!"

"Certainly!" replied Markham after only the briefest of hesitations. He turned and swept Lucinda up into his arms. She let out a muted shriek and slipped an arm around his neck to balance herself. He was momentarily surprised at how easily he had lifted her, for she was tall enough to reach the level of his ear. She smelled sweet as fresh flowers and something stirred within him as he held her close. This woman he was holding now belonged to him. It was a strange feeling.

She turned to look at him, her face rosy with embarrassment. He moved his head to give her a quick kiss on the lips and stepped forward with her over the threshold, depositing her gently in the entrance hall to the delight of the servants who gave a muted cheer.

"Well done, Markham!" said Millicent laughingly. Then taking her sister by the arm she said: "Come on, Lucy, don't look so dumbstruck! We're parched and Mrs. Potters has laid out the most delicious tea in this ever so grand drawing room. And you, my dear, have to pour, seeing you're the lady of the house!"

Lucinda found herself being led into a large room with a magnificent view of rolling lawns and a lake. It was stylishly decorated in tones of blue and grey and favored a classical style. I shall bring sunshine into this room, Lucinda found herself thinking. Perhaps a bright floral cushion here and there, or -

"Stop daydreaming and pour the tea!" insisted Milly. The children had already been helped to some delicious-looking pastries. Lucinda handed Milly a cup and then noticed that the gentlemen had gathered in the far corner nearest a huge fireplace. Smithson was busying himself with a clink of glasses. There was the pop of a champagne cork.

"Perhaps a toast first!" said Markham as he came towards them with two brimming glasses. "Lucy?" She smiled as she took the glass from him. He had called her by the pet family name.

"Thank you, Mark!" she replied with a smile and he threw back his head and laughed, a rich, amused laugh that made Smithson, the old butler, purse his lips in the suppression of a smile. Oh, yes, he had been right to suggest this union. Not that he would take all the credit when he retold the story to Mrs. Potters, for it must seem that his lordship had known the lady for a while. His lordship had specifically asked him to say this, should anyone ask.

So champagne was drunk. Charles made a speech which was both witty and sincere in his good wishes. Alfred toasted the bride. Millicent insisted on saying a word and became almost tearful in her delight that they could stay on at Hedgefield Manor. Markham cut her short by saying dryly that he could not yet afford to be a henpecked husband, so his wife's relatives would always be his chief concern. There was laughter, more champagne, tea, and pastries.

Lucinda laughed a great deal and nibbled bits of food passed to her, eating a little of everything.

"My goodness, we should be getting home!" exclaimed Alfred suddenly jumping up. "I believe you have more guests arriving shortly!"

"You will spend the night with us, won't you, Charlie?" enquired Millicent.

"Might as well kill two birds with one stone," agreed Charlie. "I leave first thing in the morning for London."

"You will let Kidson drive you in the chaise?" asked Markham, leaning back in his chair as he looked at his friend. He had removed his jacket and his shirt was unbuttoned at the collar.

"Thank you, yes!" said Charles.

"I'll just collect the children!" said Millicent rising as her husband took her hand. "They have been exploring to their hearts' content!"

Soon the group was once more on the front landing, joined now by Sarah Greenley, who had spent a pleasant hour or two chatting in the butler's pantry. To judge by her rosy complexion, observed Lucinda with a smile, they had also been toasting the success of the marriage and in more than tea! Now there was a quick hug for Lucinda from Millicent, Alfred and even Charles, and handshakes all round for the men, though Millicent gave her new brother-in-law a kiss on the cheek and a word in the ear. He nodded with a grin. The children gave their aunt and new uncle sticky kisses and the coach was off, becoming smaller and smaller as it ascended the rise.

Lucinda took a deep breath and glanced up at her new husband. He had a hand on her arm, almost as if he expected her to run away, she thought with a suppressed giggle. However, his expression was casual, as he turned to her.

"You will, no doubt want to see our rooms," he said, "and perhaps have a rest before facing my side of the family, whom, I believe, preferred to spend the night at the Royal Arms!" He tucked her hand through the crook of his arm and without another word led her up the staircase. It was a beautiful staircase of dark wood with a deep shine from many years of polishing and care. Lucinda said not a word as he swept her to the right, past portraits of stern-looking ancestors, to the south wing.

"I thought it would be best if you shared my rooms," he said after a while. "It is important to give a show of conjugal compatibility, especially when my step-mother arrives! And I have never agreed with a married couple leading separate lives!" He opened a door into a large comfortable bedroom with windows that faced the same direction as the drawing room below.

"This is lovely!" exclaimed Lucinda as she walked over to the windows. The windows flanked a paneled door which opened onto a small balcony. Then she turned to survey the rest of the room. It was dominated by a huge four-poster bed with deep blue curtains and gold tassels.

"Your dressing-room," Markham was saying as he indicated a smaller room with high cupboards to the left. There was a white basin and water-jug on a light grey marble-topped stand and a hip-bath in the same grey marble. His own dressing-room was to the right.

Immediately to the right of that was a door leading to a small cozy room which contained a fireplace, a writing table, a couch and two easy chairs covered in a rich blue fabric and a bookshelf with rows of well-worn books and catalogues. "A useful escape for when one's house is full of guests!" explained Markham with a smile. "It is part of the tower. These stairs," he added indicating a short flight of wooden stairs that spiraled higher, "take you to the top of the tower." He turned to look at her. "You would no doubt like to change and rest a while?" he asked hesitantly.

He did not seem as sure of himself now that they were alone. Lucinda suddenly felt some of her nervousness leave her. He was just as uncertain as she, and obviously not looking forward to the next lot of visitors. It was difficult for them both. "Shall I send your maid to you? I think your clothes will have been unpacked in this cupboard." Lord Markham flung open one of the doors in her dressing room. Then he kneeled down with a frown on his handsome face. "Are some of these clothes yours?" he asked.

Lucinda hurried over and put her hand to her mouth. Her sister had passed on three dresses which now lay in a crumpled heap at the bottom of the cupboard, each one having been slashed cruelly with a knife or pair of scissors. She nodded dumbly. "Milly gave them to me," she said softly.

Lord Markham strode swiftly to the door and pulled on the bell-rope. Within a minute there was a knock on the door. Biggs appeared and stepped inside. His lips tightened angrily when he saw what Lord Markham showed him.

"We'll find the culprit, Sir!" he said adamantly.

A sudden flash crossed Lord Markham's face. "Is the baby safe?" he asked.

"Very!" Biggs reassured him. "She be in the West tower with her nanny and we have five retired men from our old unit on duty."

"Thank you, Harry!" exclaimed Lord Markham, giving his corporal a quick hug. "So no one knows about her yet?"

"Correct, Sir!" nodded Harry Biggs, standing to attention. Then Lucinda could not stop herself. She quickly gave the rather amused corporal a hug as well. Lord Markham smiled with relief. Biggs gave a short bow and left the room, intent on his mission.

"We seem to have an enemy in our midst," said Lord Markham quite grimly. "I am going to suggest, my love, that you stay with me, until we have dealt with my crafty relatives. They are the only ones to gain by spoiling our future!"

"Thank you, Mark," replied Lucinda bravely.

"I am going down to the library to check on a few things, and there are quite a number of comfortable chairs if you want to rest." he added.

"I'd love to see the library!" exclaimed Lucinda. "However, I think I should just first go and confirm the menu for our evening meal. And - goodness! I do have a change of clothing after all! Our 'snipper' didn't notice my favorite gold dress which was hung behind my coat!"

"As soon as you can, come and meet me in the library, Lucy!" replied Markham with a smile. "I need to check on the accounts while I am free for a while. They say new wives can keep one very occupied!" He gave a mischievous laugh at the somewhat delightful expression of surprise on her face, and left the room.

Lucinda unhooked the gold dress from its hanger. She carefully stepped out of her green dress and hung it behind her coat. She slipped the gold dress over her head. Why - the ribbons in her hair were perfect!

She stole another glance at herself in the mirror. In this dress she looked the part of the mistress of a large mansion. She would make a success of the path she had chosen, she declared to her reflection!

She would find out more about her husband, his likes and dislikes! She would prepare his favorite meals, talk to him on subjects of his choice and when they retired to these rooms at night, she would, well, she would simply have to try her best to be what he desired!

She would do anything rather than accept a passive role while her husband paid attention to others! Her husband! The handsome Markham Elsworth – her husband! This was all too much like a fantasy! She should perhaps not have had so much champagne to drink - she needed to think. She sank back onto the comfortable bed and allowed herself to drift off into a world of swirling dreams.

She woke with a start half an hour later. Had she actually been asleep? Lucinda jumped up and smoothed her hair and skirt. She peered into the mirror and shrugged. Not too much damage done.

She had better call on the housekeeper. She could probably ring for her - Mrs. Potters, wasn't it - but she felt too restless. With a deep breath, a firm step and her chin held high, Lucinda, the new Lady Elsworth, stepped out into the corridor and made her way in the direction of the main staircase.

With the aid of a helpful footman she found herself in the region of the pantry and the kitchens where a slightly flustered Mrs. Potters presented her with suggestions for the evening menu.

"I think you have made a good selection, Mrs. Potters," said Lucinda. "Slices of melon and a cheese soufflé will be a fitting light repast after our wedding celebration with my family! Do you perhaps have some stewed plums or peaches as dessert? And perhaps some cold, sliced ham should our evening guests prefer it."

"We have both, milady," said Mrs. Potters drawing herself up proudly.

"And, Mrs. Potters, I think we should find a more suitable location for your table. Do you not find the corner of the pantry somewhat dingy?"

"Well, with your permission, milady, there is the old laundry room just next door."

"Let's see," said Lucinda briskly. Mrs. Potters reached for a key from the bunch on a loop around her waist and opened the adjoining door. "An excellent idea, Mrs. Potters!" declared Lucinda. "We shall remove a shelf or two, add a larger window to catch the morning sun, brighten it up with new curtains and you will have a room fitting for the housekeeper of such a large establishment. I shall, of course, keep the main lists and accounts at a desk of my own, no doubt in the library or one of the morning rooms, but I am sure you need space for your recipes and in order to prepare menus."

"This will be very suitable, milady," replied Mrs. Potters, her cheeks pink with pleasure. Now here was a welcome change, to be sure, thought Mrs. Potters to herself. Why the previous mistress had dismissed any suggestions she made with a sour expression! "And thank you, milady!" Lucinda inclined her head with a smile. She was curious to visit the kitchens, but perhaps she should leave that till the morning. She had perhaps better just check with Markham to confirm the use of the old laundry and the suggested changes.

Once again the watchful footman seemed to materialize from nowhere (had he been commissioned to watch for her?) and with a bow led the way towards the library. Here and there a candelabra had already been lit to brighten a corner as the evening began to stretch its fingers across the landscape. Lucinda hardly had time to take in the shadowy forms of pieces of furniture, much of it Georgian, or wonder about doorways leading to unknown rooms before they were once again at the foot of the staircase. To the right lay the library.

"This way, milady -" began the footman, when the library door was flung open rather suddenly to reveal a rather indignant-looking Smithson, one hand on the handle and the other arm flung forward to usher out a gentleman. In the background Lucinda could see Markham leaning against the mantelpiece, a scowl of irritation on his face.

The portly gentleman turned. It was George Bistow! And to judge by the sudden whiff, Bistow had either been celebrating or drowning his sorrows!

"Ah, the lady herself!" he began, his watery blue eyes gleaming as he shuffled over. "His 'igh an' mighty lordship refused to call ye! But I knew ye would come to me!"

"I think you are somewhat confused, Mr. Bistow," said Lucinda firmly, "I had no idea you were here. And it seems that Smithson is about to show you out!" She stepped back as Bistow reached out and clutched at her hand. Hardly had she snatched back her hand than Markham was at her side.

"Don't lay a hand on my wife," he said in a quiet but icy tone, as he drew Lucinda away.

"Your wife!" spat out Bistow. "She was meant to be mine! All mine! I won her fair and square! Isn't that right, Miss Lucinda?"

Lucinda recoiled in horror and clutched her husband's arm. "What utter foolishness!" she exclaimed wrathfully.

"As I told you, Bistow," Markham said coldly, "I have absolutely no interest in the card games you may or may not have played with my wife's late uncle. If you were sober right now I would personally throw you out. As it is you are no fit sight for a lady. Corbett," Markham addressed the footman, "Mr. Bistow is just leaving."

"Yes, milord!" replied the footman with alacrity as he neatly frog-marched a protesting Bistow out of a side door.

"Smithson, see that we're not disturbed. We'll have our tea in the library. Just let us know when my -er relatives arrive."

Markham took Lucinda by the arm and led her into the library, closing the door behind them.

"I'm - I'm so sorry," began Lucinda. "I have no idea what he is talking about!" First Joe and now this! What must Markham think of her? Markham said nothing for a moment as he poured wine into a goblet and handed it to her.

"Here, you probably need this," he said dryly and indicated that she sit down. He stood with an elbow on the mantelpiece, sipping his wine. The look in his eyes was hard to read. "How well do you know Bistow?" he asked.

"Just as one of my uncle's guests," replied Lucinda stiffly.

"Did he come courting you as he claims?" asked Markham with a tinge of sarcasm.

"Certainly not!" replied Lucinda hotly. "I would never have accepted the attentions of a man like him!"

"Your uncle seemed to think otherwise," suggested Markham watching her face flush with indignation.

"My uncle used to - drink too much wine at times," said Lucinda, her cheeks pink with humiliation.

"And Bistow never proposed to you?" went on Markham as he sat down opposite her.

"No!" exclaimed Lucinda. "He did -" and she swallowed with embarrassment, "he did talk to Sarah, my housekeeper, at my uncle's funeral. Something about visiting me as soon as it was decent to do so. But I would rather have run away than marry him!" she exclaimed angrily.

"Perhaps you would have run away to Thackeray," suggested Markham smoothly.

Lucinda's eyes flashed with defiant tears. "I don't think you have any right to say that!" She rose to her feet in agitation.

"Well, he seemed very concerned about you outside the church!" replied Markham as he watched her speculatively.

"As I have already told you," replied Lucinda as she twirled to face him, the gold skirt swishing around her ankles, "he was - an acquaintance - I used to occasionally visit his mother. I have no interest at all in the man! He is rough and rude!"

"But he had - he has - an interest in you?" went on Markham smoothly, his face devoid of expression.

Lucinda gave a shrug and took a deep breath as she forced herself to calm down. She knew that how she reacted now was of utmost importance. She swallowed back a sob that threatened to rise in her throat. Then, with a small smile, she picked up her glass of wine. "No doubt there are a number of ladies who still have an interest in you, Markham?"

Markham looked at her sharply, then chuckled. "*Touché*, my lady!" he replied. He raised his glass. "A toast, to our first disagreement!"

"A toast!" replied Lucinda with a smile that trembled on her lips.

Markham stepped closer and raised his left hand to her chin. He looked straight into her eyes. They were an interesting shade of green, he noted. Darker at the edges. Lucinda looked back into his deep blue eyes, holding his glance, though she felt herself coloring under his scrutiny.

"I know we have a long way to go in getting to know each other, Lucy," he said quietly, "and I know the future of Elsworth Towers depends on us, but I don't think I could ever share my wife with anyone else!"

"I don't think I could ever share my husband with anyone else," replied Lucinda evenly.

Markham pursed his lips and his expression was inscrutable. Then he raised a mocking eyebrow. "So we're stuck with each other!" he said with a chuckle as he strolled over to the hearth. "I think we shall grow to understand each other," he replied with a sidelong glance at her.

Lucinda felt her heart flutter and her lips parted as she took a breath. "Yes, I am sure you're right!" she replied rather breathlessly. She raised the wine glass to her lips and found her hand trembling.

"But, we don't have to rush into things," said Markham with a boyish grin that lit up his face for a moment. "Come, you sit here, or over here if you prefer." He directed her to an easy chair near the fire. "Now, where is old Smithson, I wonder!" He gave Lucinda a mischievous wink as the old butler made a smooth entrance at just that moment. "Always available when I need you, aren't you, Smithson? Always waiting in the wings?"" said Markham with exaggerated politeness.

"I try to be, milord," replied Smithson, with a disapproving sniff. Though, of course, one could forgive a little levity in front of his new wife. He beckoned the two footmen forward and they laid out the tea tray on a low table that Smithson had drawn up.

"Thank you," said Markham. Smithson hovered to refill their wine glasses. "You may leave the wine decanter at my elbow, Smithson. I shall assist my wife if she wishes for more."

"Well, if you're sure, milord - milady?" Lucinda smiled and nodded. "I suppose it's not every day that I have the privilege of seeing you married, milord!" replied the old man with a suppressed smile. "And I feel I have almost had a hand in it all!"

"Quite so, Smithy!" replied Markham hastily.

"What did he mean by that?" asked Lucinda with a twinkle as she watched the old man leave the room as silently as he entered, though she could swear he was chuckling to himself.

"Oh, Smithy has this notion that he has to keep an eye on me and give me advice!" replied Markham evasively. "Will you serve yourself, or can I assist?"

"Oh, no, let me serve you!" replied Lucinda hastily, blushing quite rosily as she went about her wifely duty.

Markham was in his shirt sleeves, his cravat loose for comfort. He leaned back in his chair, legs stretched out before him, quietly watching this woman who was now his wife. What did he really know about her? She would look the part dressed perhaps a little more fashionably than at present, although the dress she was wearing was lovely and revealed enough of her fine figure. The firelight caught the gleams of auburn lights in her hair.

She had fine features - and a perfect mouth, one which would probably make most men think of claiming in a kiss. Men like Bistow, or Thackeray? Were there perhaps others? In a small community like this Lucinda certainly would have been a good catch as a wife. He wondered why she had not married yet. Or had she set her sights higher than the average farmer? But he was being unfair. She had had her responsibilities with her sister and her uncle. And she had scarcely set about entrapping him! This was all his doing; of that there was no doubt at all.

He wondered about the true nature of her involvement with Thackeray. No doubt rumors would reach him soon enough if there were any substance. Bistow was not a problem! She obviously loathed him.

"Oh, sorry, what's that?" said Markham as Lucinda looked at him enquiringly. He leaned forward to accept a side-plate of sliced melon.

"I was just saying that you and Charles appear to have known each other for a while."

"Indeed," replied Markham, "our fathers were friends and we studied together."

Lucinda sat down and began to eat small bits of the tasty repast. She had not eaten much earlier. She sipped the wine that Smithson had poured her. Its warmth seemed to spread through her. Then she rose to pour their tea.

"Have you met his fiancé, Catherine?" went on Markham conversationally as he took a forkful of soufflé. Lucinda shook her head and Markham went into some detail to describe the budding romance, rather amazed himself that he remembered so much. "I actually introduced them," he said with a grin. "We were at a masked ball last New Year Eve, when I noticed Charlie's eyes fixed on this rather diminutive blonde-haired lady dressed as a shepherdess. I duly asked her to dance the waltz and then feigned a sore ankle and passed her on to Charlie! He was initially dumbstruck and fairly speechless, but she made up for that! They fell in love, they say, without seeing each other's faces! Now that is what I call true love!" added Markham with a short laugh.

"Yes, indeed!" replied Lucinda. "A meeting of souls!"

"Do you believe in soul-mates?" asked Markham, a far-away look in his eyes.

"I think so - perhaps after a while of being acquainted," replied Lucinda, noting his expression. Was he referring to a lady of his acquaintance?

"Perhaps you're right," said Markham coming out of his reverie. "I think, however, that trust must play a crucial role," he added conversationally. "One cannot truly love unless one can trust as well."

"Certainly," agreed Lucinda.

The light meal passed companionably enough. Markham had a way of asking questions that were not in the least threatening, and soon Lucinda found herself telling him all about her late parents and the good memories she had of them. He could sense the love she had had for them and for a moment his own heart ached for the mother he had lost and who could have been part of his life.

"More wine?" asked Markham after she briefly told of their demise. When she declined, he rose to his feet.

At that very moment, Smithson appeared at the door. "Your relatives are in the drawing room, milord!" he said steadily, but certainly not cheerfully. "And milady, this is a note for you from the parson's wife."

Lucinda took the note from Smithson and opened it quickly. Then she stepped over to Lord Markham, succeeding in controlling her expression. It read: *'My dearest Lucinda - please inform Markham that my very impulsive husband, Arthur, has just returned from London. He rode through the night with one of our deacons, to lodge your marriage certificate with the proper authorities. Charles was accosted by two villains just inside the church door. Luckily, I found him, having left my shawl at the organ! The authorities have the originals as the copies Charles had were taken. Please do not be concerned! Arthur regards himself as the hero of the day! We shall visit soon. Love and best wishes from your friend, Jenny.'*

"They're trying everything to stop us!" muttered Markham fiercely under his breath.

"Is everything in order, milord?" asked a concerned Smithson.

"Perfect!" replied Markham with a nod and small smile. "Please just ask Biggs to come to the library before we go down to greet our guests. Get someone to give them some refreshment while they wait," he added somewhat carelessly.

"So that accounts for the bruise!" exclaimed Lucinda. "I thought perhaps Charles had fallen and hurt himself."

"I was remiss!" confessed Markham. "I meant to enquire, but he seemed at ease. None of us realized that our opponents would go to that length of trying to delay the lodging of our legal documents."

A moment later, Biggs appeared at the door of the library. Lord Markham swiftly explained the situation and warned him to be extra vigilant and to report anything strange. Biggs nodded firmly.

Then it seemed as if Lord Markham had made up his mind. "Please ask Susan's nanny to dress her suitably and bring her down in an hour or so to me. My wife hasn't even met her yet, but I have no doubts as to her love for children!"

Lucinda blushed happily and, taking Markham's hand, they smilingly went down the stairs in the direction of the main reception area.

Chapter 8

Lord Markham nodded and then held out his arm for Lucinda. He felt her arm trembling slightly and he murmured: "I know them very well, never fear!"

Lucinda smiled and squeezed his arm gratefully. There was only one thing for it - pretend that she was in control.

The tinkling laughter of a lady, was hushed as they entered. There was a moment's silence as four pairs of eyes stared at her.

"Why Mark, do introduce me to our guests!" Lucinda said gaily. He bowed briefly as he lifted her hand to his lips, his smile affable, yet she could see the flicker of amusement in his glance.

"Certainly, my love," he said smoothly. "Lucinda, this is my step-mamma, Amelia." The lady in question lifted her brows and looked at Lucinda with an expression that could only be described as disdain. She was over middle age, yet dressed in flounces reminiscent of the present French fashion that befitted someone much younger. Her hair was dressed in an amazing style that added at least a foot and a half to her height! The shades of pink in her outfit somehow made Lucinda think of the pudding Sarah often made!

"My half-brother, Lawrence," went on Markham. Lucinda put out her hand and the young man, of rather foppish appearance in a purple and yellow waistcoat that glittered with a row of small diamond buttons, brushed her fingers with his lips and a mutter of: "Charmed, I'm sure!"

"And this is Miss Melissa Jordan." Lucinda found herself gazing down into a pair of bright blue eyes set in a rather wide, yet attractive face, framed by rolls of golden hair looped with cords and ribbons, obviously set in the latest fashion. She was wearing a light yellow afternoon dress that clung to her rather ample breasts like a second skin and fluffed out into a billowy over-skirt of the same material.

"Oh, Markham!" she laughed with the tinkling laugh Lucinda had heard before. "Surely you should call us very old friends! Perhaps even more than that!"

Markham simply inclined his head. "My wife - Lucinda," he drawled as he led her to a seat near the window where he joined her.

Lucinda sat down as gracefully as she could and smiled cheerfully at her husband. That hussy would not get the better of her! She would have felt so much better had she known what a delightful picture she made with the morning sun catching her auburn hair which had been brushed to a sheen.

Melissa Jordan's eyes narrowed. This could not be happening! She had hardly returned to London when she had been dragged along post haste by Amelia and the odious Lawrence, who for some reason had insisted that Markham would want to marry her just as soon as he could. Somehow this would be very good for them, for then they would be able to make him agree to certain conditions. And now - here they were - at first not able to take in the news that a wedding had taken place the previous day - and here was his bride, smiling as if she owned the place - dressed in a ridiculous outfit that was dated and clung to her body, set to catch Markham's attention, a fact which she had no doubt carefully planned! Well, there was more than one way of breaking a marriage!

Melissa smiled her sweetest smile. "But, Mark, don't tell me your bride is unknown to us?"

"Hardly," replied Markham blandly. We have been neighbors for many years."

"You have?" said Lady Amelia with a puzzled smirk. "From which side of the village?"

"I grew up next door!" replied Lucinda cheerfully. "Markham and I knew each other as children!"

"I don't remember that," said Amelia spitefully. "You left home to live elsewhere, didn't you, Markham. I remember how upset your father was."

"Lucy and I met before that," replied Markham with a shrug.

"And we never forgot each other!" added Lucinda mischievously. "But, how remiss of me! What about refreshment?"

"We rang for some half an hour ago," replied Amelia coldly. "Really, Markham, I think it's about time you got rid of your old butler. He is obviously way past retirement!"

"But there is no haste is there?" asked Lucinda politely, restraining her tongue as she noticed Markham's mouth set in a hard line. Just then Smithson ushered in two footmen, carrying trays laden with refreshments. Lucinda rose to her feet and indicated where the trays should be deposited. She felt Markham's gaze on her. She should have stayed seated, she supposed. But force of habit and agitation at Amelia's remarks had made her rise.

She murmured her thanks to the footmen, gave Smithy a warm smile and assured him she would see to the pouring of the tea. At least she had had practice enough at that! She glanced up to see a smirk on Melissa's face and taking a deep breath she forced her hands to relax. They would not see that her stomach was a mass of butterflies! She would get through this ordeal somehow.

Soon all the preferences for milk or lemon had been dealt with and slices of vanilla cake dealt out. Then Lucinda sat back with her own tea. Melissa was laughing her tinkling laugh as she quizzed Lawrence about the latest fashion of necktie which he was sporting, Amelia was sipping her tea with distaste and looking around the room as if she had left something of value somewhere. Markham was leaning back in his chair with an air of boredom, though his dark blue eyes seemed to miss not a thing.

"Oh, but you must come up for the season, Mark!" Melissa was saying. "It just won't be the same without you!" She was all smiles and dimples as she inclined her head prettily.

"Markham will no doubt be too busy with his new wife!" replied Lawrence with a smothered laugh. He had been enjoying the attention he had received from Melissa.

"Oh, don't be naughty, Lawrence!" exclaimed Melissa with another tinkle, noticing the way Markham paused and allowed his gaze to flicker without humor over his rather rude half-brother. "Markham's new wife is used to the country. She will, no doubt, find herself too busy getting used to running Elsworth Towers!"

"She will certainly need a new wardrobe if she does show her face in London, Markham," said Amelia disdainfully. "Past fashion is all very well in royalty, but will hardly pass in polite society!"

Lucinda felt the color rise to her cheeks. How dare they speak about her as if she were not even present! With an effort she controlled the retort that sprang to her lips. She managed to incline her head with a tight smile. Markham said not a word. At least he could have said something! He had got her into this situation after all!

"Oh, my, she's blushing!" exclaimed Melissa with a laugh. "Poor thing! Dear Markham, where *did* you find her!"

JUST THEN SMITHSON interrupted with: "Excuse me, milord, there's a Dr. Jenner here who said he was requested to call."

Markham nodded and rose to his feet. "Is one of the staff poorly, Smithson?"

"Not to my knowledge, milord!" replied Smithson.

"Oh, that is Thomas Jenners!" exclaimed Lady Amelia, beckoning the doctor in with what she probably considered a glittering smile.

"Are you not well, Amelia?" asked Lord Markham as he took in the scene, still standing.

"Oh, I am very well, Markham!" replied Lady Amelia with some sarcasm at his use of her name. "It's just for the sake of following procedure! I am sure you are aware that your father's will had a codicil."

Markham nodded, his face inscrutable, while the so-called Dr. Jenner moved uncomfortably from one foot to the other.

"I was informed that you both spent the night at the Parson's house?" said Lady Amelia with a triumphant look. "I hardly think that would be the place to consummate a marriage!" Both Melissa and Lawrence sniggered.

"What are you saying, Amelia?" asked Lord Markham with the slightest of smiles.

"According to centuries of procedure, the bride must be checked just to make sure that the marriage is legal - otherwise it is easily annulled!"

Lord Markham turned round and looked at Lucinda. Then they both began to laugh. Markham bent down to kiss her on her lips, then added: "We actually did not spend the night at the parsonage. And after last night, both my wife and I find this somewhat amusing!"

"B-but.." stammered Lady Amelia.

Smithson had stepped outside the room. In his place stood the sturdy Biggs, his eyes glistening with anticipation.

"I'm sorry, Dr. Jenner, but your services will not be required!" said Markham politely. "Biggs, would you show the gentleman out, and while you're at it, just check what he is carrying in his black medical bag."

"Yes, Sir!" replied Biggs as he firmly marched the protesting man down the corridor towards the front door.

Lord Markham took his seat once again.

"Anyone for a second cup of tea?" asked Lucinda asked with a lingering smile.

Just then, Biggs returned and handed the black bag to Markham who took a quick peek, The bag was full of money and the butt of a pistol glinted in one corner.

"Thanks, Biggs," replied Markham quietly. "Please put this in the library for me. Oh, and just check if Adam is on duty." Adam was one of the retired members of the military unit who was now part of those guarding the castle. Biggs gave a short bow and left.

"What was that all about?" asked Lawrence.

"It seems that someone bribed the so-called doctor," said Markham calmly, crossing his legs.

"I think you are making a terrible mistake, Markham!" replied Lady Amelia looking slightly flustered. "The whole of London is expecting you and Melissa to wed!"

"No one heard that from my lips," said Markham with a glare at his step-mother. "Is there anything else I can help you with?"

"I hardly think so!" exclaimed Melissa angrily as she rose to her feet with a swirl of puffy skirts. Lawrence got up as well and then went to help his mother to her feet.

"Smithson will show you out," said Markham with a nod. "And I shall have another cup of tea, my love!" he said with his special smile to Lucinda.

Lucinda got up as the others strode towards the door where Smithson was waiting. Then Amelia turned and looked straight at Markham as if her were precious to her.

“Marriages can be annulled, you know,” went on Amelia lowering her voice confidentially. “A mere two months ago, young Fauntleroy had his marriage annulled. You know, Joseph Nobel’s boy.”

“But he’d married someone who was already married, mother!” put in Lawrence, earning a glare from his mother and a flicker of annoyance from Melissa.

MARKHAM UNCROSSED HIS legs and sat up in his chair. He leaned forward, pursing his lips, his elbows on his knees, his fingers tapping one another lightly. Anyone who really knew Markham would have read the danger signals, but Amelia leaned forward even more conspiratorially.

"You could give her a settlement of sorts and then you would be free to follow your heart!" she whispered dramatically.

Markham rose to his feet. He strode over to the fireplace and turned abruptly. "Can I make myself clear to all present," he began evenly. "I appreciate your concern for my welfare, late in the day though it might be." He paused to let his blue gaze rest on his step-mamma for a moment. "But, be assured that I have married the woman of my choice and there is nothing that you or anyone can say or do to change that. Surely I have a right to choose, or is there some ulterior motive for the concern displayed today?" He glanced sharply at his stepmother who was trying to look hurt and affronted.

"Oh, come, Mark, don't be angry," said Melissa as she suddenly stepped towards him, and taking his arm, led him to the window. "You know how much we care about you and we're frankly just a little surprised, that's all, at your decision to marry so hastily and someone quite unknown!" She leaned closer to him and rested her head against his shoulder, her gold curls against his cheek. "Shouldn't an old friend show concern, especially when we were such good friends once," she whispered just loudly enough for him to hear.

"Oops!" said Lucinda innocently, as she quickly turned the spout of the teapot away from Melissa's foot.

"You clumsy creature!" exclaimed Melissa angrily hopping sideways, even as Markham smothered a laugh.

"So sorry!" said Lucinda sweetly as the trio at last exited the door.

"Come here, my beautiful clumsy creature!" said Markham, as he put both his arms around her, continuing to chuckle with mirth.

Lucinda found herself laughing too, especially when Markham said: "Pity the doctor had already left!"

Then Markham suddenly called out: "Lawrence! Are you still here?"

His half-brother appeared in the doorway, looking rather startled. "What - what is it, Markham?"

"I just wanted to mention this: you are and always will be my brother. So, if you ever want to come for a visit, or get tired of London, just let us know!" He stepped forward and Lawrence embraced him almost emotionally.

"Thank you, Markham!" he replied in a voice that trembled slightly. "And I think you have married an amazing woman!" With that he smiled at Lucinda and turned quickly to follow the others.

"Nice boy!" commented Lucinda with a grin. Markham gave her another hug and just hid a smile.

Chapter 9

Then she looked up with a start. In the doorway stood Biggs, looking very grim.

"What is it?" asked Markham swiftly.

"Someone has taken Susan! Smithson's sister is in a state. The new young lady who was supposed to be training as a lady's maid, came to fetch her, saying Lady Lucinda had asked her to bring the child! The nanny was warned that you might want to see the child, so let her go!"

"Right!" replied Markham. "Send out the alert - all our guys - and I'll get my riding boots!"

"Sir - if I may say so - it may be a diversion! Lady Lucinda must take care!" replied Biggs earnestly.

"Lucinda," said Markham decisively. "I want you to stay in the library! Smithson will bring you refreshment and we'll put you, Biggs, at the door - armed! If there is any disturbance, hide in the little back room where my documents are, my love, and lock yourself in!"

Lucinda nodded, gave her husband a swift kiss on the cheek and headed for the library. Biggs passed on Markham's message to the men and then descended to the library. "Lady Lucinda!" he called out at the door. "If I want to come in for some reason, I shall knock and say: 'It's the merry month of May!' If I just knock and say it's Biggs - don't open the door, but hide! Did you hear that, milady?"

"Thank you, Biggs, I did!" replied Lucinda as she went to look out the window anxiously. Who could have taken the baby, Susan? This was terrible! Then she curled up in an armchair out of sight of the windows and said a quiet prayer for help for the little one she had not even yet seen!

Meanwhile, Abe, who had always taken care of Lucinda's horse, Firefly, had just returned from a gentle gallop and was preparing to brush the horse down. He looked up from behind the tree where he had dismounted. A rather shabby-looking buggy had drawn up, pulled by two just as shabby-looking horses.

Then he saw the slim figure of one of the maids running towards it. In her arms she was holding a child, which was whimpering slightly! No - she was taking Lord Elsworth's adopted daughter to the buggy! The news about the child was almost a secret, but news eventually leaked to servants in a house.

Abe quietly remounted Firefly and began to follow the buggy at a safe distance. At first he thought it could be on its ways to London, which would complicate matters. He was not familiar with London! But then the buggy turned left onto a country road. A small cloud of dust followed it, so Abe carefully steered Firefly onto the verge of the road which was grassy. There was a farmhouse ahead and that was where the buggy stopped.

He turned Firefly behind the trees and watched as the maid alighted with the child, which was now crying quite loudly, in her arms. She ran up the pathway into the farmhouse and the door slammed behind her. The man who was driving the buggy unharnessed the horses and entered the house.

Abe moved Firefly carefully deeper into the forest, dismounted and whispered to the horse to be silent. What should he do now? He could not leave, as the people might just be calling here briefly with the child. Or were they going to ask for a ransom? He knew one thing! He had to rescue the little one very soon!

He waited very patiently as the sun began to set and Firefly contentedly cropped the grass around her. He had to get closer to the house to see where the child was! And how on earth would he carry the baby while riding Firefly?

He could do it if he looped a blanket into a sling around his chest and held her with one arm! He had seen one of the farmers do that with his own little son.

As soon as it was dusk, Abe rested Firefly's reins over the branch of a tree and began to move towards the house stealthily. There was a light in what appeared to be a kitchen. At a table sat a man with a large glass of ale, while the maid dished food from a pot onto his plate.

Abe quietly circled round to the back of the small house. He peered into a window. It was a bedroom, but that was all he could see. The next window was slightly open. He held his breath and peered in carefully. Lying, on her side, fast asleep, lay the little one!

Without hesitation, Abe carefully and quietly raised the old window. He deftly climbed over the sill. Then he gently lifted the child who was wrapped in a blanket. In her mouth was a dummy which she sucked on comfortably as she slept.

With gentle hands he carried the little one back through the window. For once he was glad he was slight of stature. Avoiding the light streaming from the front window, he made his way, step by step towards the spot where he had tethered Firefly.

He mounted the horse with the baby held close to his side. Then as she wriggled a bit, he tied a firm knot in the blanket that held her and put the loop over his own head so that she rested on his chest. With one hand on the reins and the child clutched to his chest, he whispered to Firefly, who raised her ears and began to walk slowly towards the road. It was almost as if she understood!

Once Abe reached the main road, he urged the horse to go faster and thus they progressed. The baby murmured sleepily, but felt secure in the firm blanket and his gentle hold. He took a short cut that he knew through the forest. Within twenty minutes he had arrived at Elseworth Estate. The moon was out and Firefly went quickly up to the gate leading to the stables.

Abe dismounted smoothly and found himself facing the old butler, Smithson, who almost burst into tears of joy when he saw the child. "You found her, you wonderful lad!" the old man said. "What happened? I was coming to fetch a horse to ride to help in the search!"

Abe quickly told what he had experienced and Smithson indicated that they should go into the shadows of the stable. "I'll tell ye what, young man," said Smithson shakily. "Take the baby up into the hay loft! I'll send my sister, the nanny, with a bottle of milk for the wee one, and she can stay here with you! Meanwhile, I shall get hold of one of the men to let his lordship know the good news! You will keep the child safe?"

"I can promise you that, Mr. Smithson!" replied Abe. He had already ascended to the loft and placed Susan on a soft bed of hay. "Anyone dangerous coming in here, will get a pitchfork in his ears!" He sat down at the top of the steps, so that he could keep an eye on the doorway and on the child.

Within five minutes, the nanny, wrapped in a dark cloak, arrived with bottles of milk and a softer blanket. She whispered her thanks and settled down beside the sleeping child. Abe crept down the stairs and took his stand under a tree outside. He still held the pitchfork in his hand.

Meanwhile Smithson was fairly flustered as he told Biggs what had occurred. "How do we let his lordship know?" he asked.

"Not yet!" murmured Biggs. "Please hide in the nearest room - now!" Biggs had heard a thud in the hallway and one of the footmen had cried out: "No!"

Three rough-looking men came up the stairs. Biggs stood flat against the passage wall where one of the pillars was slightly extended as part of the architecture. As the men began to walk past him, he kicked the first in the small of his back and then grabbed the two shorter men, knocking their heads soundly together! All were groaning on the floor as Smithson suddenly emerged from a small drawing room, in his hands a long chord that had been used to tie up the curtains. Biggs gave each man a hearty kick against the head and then expertly tied their arms behind their backs. He pursed his lips to a low, but piercing whistle, and within a few seconds, two of the retired unit, Adams and Cochran, were with him. They hoisted all three men up and swiftly took them out the front door and tied each to a tree with wire that they had found in the woodshed when Biggs had told them to be prepared for anything!

Then, to Smithson's amazement, Biggs took out a short pistol-shaped object and shot two blue flares into the sky. They shone and twisted and then fell slowly to earth.

It was that signal which made Markham's heart race happily. His men had done their job! Two flares meant that both Lucinda and Susan were safe.

He wheeled his big black stallion and, followed by one of his footmen, who had trained with horses and was riding a dappled horse that had belonged to Markham's father, headed for the Royal Arms Inn.

Once they arrived there, Markham indicated that William, the footman, stay with the horses, while he strode inside. The person occupying the desk in the entrance, who also owned the inn, quickly recognized his lordship and with a smile led him down the corridor where his relatives had rented rooms.

The innkeeper knocked politely on one of the doors. It was opened by Lawrence, who looked surprised to see his brother. But Amelia called over his shoulder: "Do come in, Markham! I was expecting you!"

Lord Markham nodded his thanks to the innkeeper and strode inside. Amelia and Melissa were partaking of some wine at a round table. Markham pulled out a chair and sat down. Lawrence continued to look puzzled as his mother smiled.

Without greeting anyone, Lord Markham said: "Well, Amelia, what's the deal? What do I have to do to get my wife and my daughter back?"

"What?" exclaimed Lawrence.

"Keep quiet and keep out of this!" snapped his mother. Lawrence folded his arms and leaned against the door.

"It's perfectly simple, Markham," replied the former Lady Amelia. "Agree to an annulment of your marriage - and I have documents for you to sign right here," she added as she leaned to the bookshelf beside her and took three legal-looking pieces of paper. "Then, we return your er- daughter, as you call her, and we send your dear Lucinda back to Hedgelands, hopefully unharmed."

Lord Markham took the legal papers and skimmed through them. Then he rose and leaned on the table and looked straight at Amelia. "If you have harmed one hair of their heads, you will be going to prison, Amelia! I have contacts in the government who owe me a great deal!"

"Oh, nonsense, Mark!" exclaimed Melissa. "You and I will deal well together!"

"Not until hell freezes over!" said Markham, glaring at her in disdain. Then he very deliberately tore the papers in pieces and flung them in the fire that was warming the room. He swung around, nodded to Lawrence to open the door, and before he left, tipped the table with its glasses of wine into the laps of both ladies!

"Lawrence! Don't just stand there!" shrieked his mother. But Lawrence had already accompanied his brother outside. He shook his hand in apology and his face lit up as Markham told him confidentially that all was well.

"See you soon!" exclaimed Lawrence as he put on his saddest expression and re-entered the inn.

When Lord Markham and his faithful William arrived back at Elsworth Estate, they were just in time to see the two men who belonged to the constabulary of the village, frog-march three rough men out to the police transportation, with the energetic help of Biggs. Corporal Biggs saluted them and they left.

Then Biggs noticed his lordship and William emerge from the shadows. He bowed and smiled at his lordship, who clasped his hand and swiftly ascended the steps leading up to the castle.

Sitting cozily in the drawing room he found Lucinda sitting on a couch. On her lap was Susan, who was curiously touching her new mother's face and gurgling in glee. She was dressed in a warm nightdress of pale pink and there was a small ribbon in her hair.

"There's Papa!" exclaimed Lucinda as she got up with the child in her arms. Quite touchingly, the little one stretched both her chubby arms towards her father. Later, Susan's nanny reported to the rest of the staff that it was the first time she had seen tears running down his lordship's cheeks as he strode over and embraced both his wife and his child.

Markham gently took his daughter onto his lap and bounced her up and down, while she looked at him, at first curiously, then a wide smile covered her little face and she clapped her tiny hands, which were as beautiful as her rosy-cheeked face.

"You've won her heart already!" exclaimed Lucinda as she gave both a kiss. Lord Markham held his lips on Lucinda's own while Susan squealed with delight and pulled on her father's ear!.

"Where will our little one sleep tonight?" asked Markham as if a sudden thought had struck him.

"With your permission, milord, we have turned the bedroom next to yours which was usually meant for the lady of the house, into a nursery! Didn't take long, so if you do not approve - " said Smithson.

"I love the idea!" exclaimed Lord Markham.

"So do I!" added Lucinda.

"If I may say so, 'twas her ladyship's idea!" said Smithson with a wide smile.

"And I reckon it's bedtime for the young lady!" interjected the nanny. "Come, Susan, kiss your papa and mama goodnight!" Everyone clapped as the child seemed to understand.

Lord Markham accepted a glass of wine from Smithson and passed it to Lucinda. Then he looked towards the door, where Biggs was standing, his eyes twinkling delightedly. "Please join us, Harry," his lordship said. "We need to hear the whole story!"

Biggs nodded in a soldierly fashion, accepted a glass of wine from Smithson with a bow and drew up an easy chair near to the couple.

Then the staff disappeared quietly, either to take up their positions on duty, or to go to bed for a well-earned rest.

Chapter 10

Markham leaned forward as he listened carefully while Harry Biggs recounted what had happened.

"We owe a great deal to that young man, Abe!" said Markham. "Harry, I want you to take him under your wing and see what his talents are! We need young men like him at Elsworth. "

"Yes, Sir!" nodded Harry Biggs enthusiastically. "And if I may say so, your Mr. Smithson must have been quite a star in his day if he can organize and think so quickly on his feet now!"

"He is a real gem!" agreed Lucinda, while Markham nodded and smiled.

"One other thing, Harry. I want you to consider moving into the rose cottage that my mother had built and decorated at the end of the garden. It has three bedrooms and plenty of space for your family!"

Harry Biggs' eyes widened. "Are you sure, Sir?" he asked in amazement. "Amy has admired that cottage for a long time now!"

"I am perfectly sure!" replied Lord Markham with a grin. "You will be closer, and your little boys will have ample space for fun and games! In a year or two they will be within walking distance from the school."

"That sounds splendid!" agreed Lucinda.

"And another thing," went on Lord Markham with a quick glance at Lucinda. "My wife will accompany me wherever I go. When I go to London for the parliamentary reports, she goes with me! Now, I know that you have a brother-in-law who is a fashion designer. Is it possible that he could spend a day or two here at Elsworth to design outfits that my wife likes? He could bring samples as well!"

"Amy, my wife, has friends in the village who are wonderful seamstresses who often work for him!" replied Harry Biggs with a smile of delight. "Milady will be the best-dressed lady in London!"

"That would be wonderful!" exclaimed Lady Lucinda with a laugh. "Not to be the best-dressed lady, but to upgrade my fairly poor wardrobe. My sister was horrified when she inspected my so-called favorite dresses! And - and of course - Susan must get some pretty little dresses too!"

Both Biggs and Lord Markham winked at each other at Lucinda's reaction. Markham's heart felt warm! How lovely to be married to someone so agreeable, attractive and unselfish!

"I think we need a good rest now, my dear," he said cheerfully as he got up. "Harry, if all is in order with the night shift, you go home and have a good rest too!"

"Thank you, milord!" grinned Harry. "Goodnight, milady, and thank you for being the person that we all need at Elsworth!" With that he was gone.

Lucinda smiled up at her husband and then leaned against him as he steered her up the stairs to their rooms.

"I wonder how many beds one can fit into a nursery?" asked Markham with a mischievous twinkle in his eyes.

"I suppose maybe as many as six, or even eight, if they are bunk-beds," replied Lucinda hiding a smile.

"What?" gasped Markham in mock horror. "You will bankrupt me, wife!"

Lord Markham and Lady Lucinda began to laugh! As they reached the door to their rooms, the staff on duty saw fit to report the following morning to the others that the couple had simply dissolved in laughter as they closed the door! What a beautiful sound it was with which to end a stressful day!

ABOUT THE AUTHOR:

I grew up on a farm in the Eastern Cape of South Africa, near a small town called Stutterheim, in view of the rolling, beautiful Amatola Mountain range. I studied at Rhodes University in Grahamstown for a BA and U.ED, and went on to teach English to high school students. I have always loved writing and began expressing myself as a teenager. I thoroughly enjoyed teaching literature and telling numerous stories to my classes. I was asked to write a series of traditional stories relating to all the eleven languages in South Africa (Lectio Publishers), and also wrote stories for school readers and libraries. My hobbies include reading, writing, poetry and art. At present, my family and I reside in Johannesburg.

Thank you for reading my book! If you enjoyed it, please take a moment to leave a review.

www.ingramcontent.com/pod-product-compliance
Ingram Content Group UK Ltd.
Pitfield, Milton Keynes, MK11 3LW, UK
UKHW040042200726
13854UKWH00001B/494

9 798201 378257